/

DILLY

DILLY

MATTHEW P. MAYO

FIVE STAR
A part of Gale, a Cengage Company

LIBRARY OF CONGRESS CATALOGING-IN-PUBLICATION DATA

Names: Mayo, Matthew P, author.
Title: Dilly / Matthew P. Mayo.
Description: First Edition. | Farmington Hills, Mich. : Five Star, a part of Gale, a Cengage Company, 2020.
Identifiers: LCCN 2019041803 | ISBN 9781432871079 (hardcover)
Subjects: GSAFD: Western stories.
Classification: LCC PS3613.A963 D55 2020 | DDC 813/.6—dc23
LC record available at https://lccn.loc.gov/2019041803

First Edition. First Printing: June 2020
Find us on Facebook—https://www.facebook.com/FiveStarCengage
Visit our website—http://www.gale.cengage.com/fivestar
Contact Five Star Publishing at FiveStar@cengage.com

Printed in Mexico
Print Number: 01   Print Year: 2020

For my friend, John D. Nesbitt

"Every traveler has a home of his own, and he learns to appreciate it the more from his wandering."

—*Charles Dickens*

PROLOGUE

Autumn, 1931

Big Horn County, Wyoming

Once again, I look back on that day so long ago when I was drawn to the Hatterson Ranch, and I shake my head. What would my life have been like if I'd kept walking? A number of people would not have died, I know that much. Some of them I cared for deeply, one in particular.

So with the view that long years give a man, if I could do it over again, would I stop at that ranch gate or would I keep on walking?

That's when I hear the stove door squawk in the kitchen, and a log being chunked into its hungry mouth, and I smile and regret my thoughts. That is my Felice, using her apron as a hot pad to shut the door, saving the fancy flowered hot pads I bought her for Christmas last year, still hanging on the hook behind the stove, never used and never would be. Too pretty, she'd said, shaking her head.

I reckon it's a good thing I was born with a keen curiosity to see what that ranch was all about, else I never would have met her.

I shift in my chair on the porch and shout through the screen door. "Hey, Felice . . . do you ever think on the sheep wars?"

I hear her footsteps, and there she is, standing on her side of the screen, drying her hands on her apron. "The past is a dead thing, Dilly. No use hauling up that sore memory from the bottom of the pond." She shakes her head and walks back to the kitchen.

I carve a fresh knob off my plug of tobacco, snap my old, worn Barlow shut, and slide it back into my vest pocket. I pick off the lint and it occurs to me how right she is.

As I chew that tobacco, savoring the sweet molasses and applewood flavors, I fold my hands over my belly and fall to musing, the perfect pastime for a lazy Sunday afternoon. As I recall, that day I came upon the Hatterson Ranch had been a Sunday, too.

Hell, even if it wasn't, it should have been.

I am not from here, I remember saying to a thin fellow in a boxcar one time, as a response to his question. I have never heard before or since a man fart so much as that skinny drink. He called it "bilious ructions," but I spent the entire time in that dank boxcar with tears in my eyes, only half of them for the situation I'd found myself in—that of traveling alone across the country. "Ain't none of us are from here, son," he'd said. "That's why it's called a frontier. Raw and woolly and untrammeled by interlopers."

I didn't understand half those words, but I drew his meaning. Back in the spring of 1893, that part of the country was indeed still untrammeled.

I have since learned the meaning of the word and I trot it out like a fairground pony now and again to impress people, mostly my wife. She'll snort and go back to her sock mending. I am hell on heels, she says. *It's because I am always looking up to you, my dearest,* I tell her. She snorts again, but I see a tiny smile on her pretty mouth.

Nowadays, of course, this part of the U.S. of A is fair to bursting with all manner of people from all over the world. You have the Chinese—a more polite and kinder people you will not meet. I am proud to count two of them as my close friends. But

I would not wish to cross them in a fight, fair or otherwise. Vengeance is mine, sayeth the Lord, and I think he learned it from a Chinaman.

Then you have the Irish, also some of the kindest folks you are likely to meet. But you get one of their breed riled or drunk (usually one leads to the other), and you best duck and run. Then there are Italians. Again, good people but a whole lot like the Irish and the Chinese. It's coming to me as I write this that folks all over the world are pretty much the same.

There was that Russian woman who ended up in these parts some years ago toting a pet rabbit and a mute little Mexican girl no more than two years of age. No one here speaks the woman's lingo, and the child, as I say, can't utter a lick, so we are left to rely on the wormy ways of our own minds to figure out her story.

But I tell you what, you have an ailment, you'd better have a deep-chested horse if you pass up her ministrations, because it's a long distance to Doc Binner's office in Greenhaven, some miles down the valley.

That Russian woman has cured more chesty croups and delivered more healthy bairns and eased more chilblains and rheumatics than anyone in Wyoming. Though I wonder if she could have gained the upper hand in a battle with that skinny fellow's bilious ructions . . .

I realize I am doing what my friend, Teapot Stover, calls generalizing. He says it's a surefire way to raise the ire of them I am generalizing about. I can't say I disagree.

But I will say one more thing about a certain people. The Basques. They are dearest to me of all the people I have met in my life. Not that I am a well-traveled man, though at one time, as a boy, I roved a long distance, only to find when I thought my traveling days had come to an end that my journeying had only begun. Different type of travel, though. I'll get to that.

As I say, the Basques mean much to me. They are without debate the smilingest, kindest people you could meet. They are also the most talented, from gentling beasts to curing their ills to singing and dancing and generally whooping it up. Most of all, they are the hardest-working folks I've ever met.

My wife says all this praise of the Basques is hogwash. Which I find odd as she is Basque. I am not, though for years I tried every day to be one. I never really will be, of course. Nowadays I only fret over things I can change, if they need changing. The rest, I tip my hat to and move along.

The Basques come from Basque Country, which is part of Spain and part of France, and while some of them are sheepherders there, I came to find out that a good many more of them are not. But as they are clever, they picked up on the skills required of that trade and set to work here in the United States.

As sheepmen, they spend months alone, far up in the summer hill country, tending vast flocks, with no company save for their dogs and all those sheep, and a visit every couple of weeks from one of their fellows bringing up supplies and scraps of news, if there's anything worth telling. Then there are the coyotes, the wolves, and bears. Hardly fit conversationalists for men.

The Basques have been called names I almost hate to mention in these pages, but I promised myself I would not shy from the bald truth in this document, and so I shall set down a few: sheepeater, muttonhead . . . There are others, but too much salt will spoil the soup.

I see I have been ricocheting off topics like a slug fired in a rock quarry. My wife says that talking with me is sometimes like chasing chickens. I am fond of chickens, especially under bubbling dumplings, and so I will take her remarks as a compliment, even though I know she intended otherwise.

When I first met the girl who would become my wife, she was grinding corn between stones, a slow, soft, dragging noise. That's how I found her. I followed that scraping sound and there she was. Prettiest girl I had ever seen.

Wore one of those peasant shirts that tie at the throat. Only hers wasn't tied and her skin at the neck and down lower was the color of Granna's tea after she'd run more water than she ought through the leaves. The thing I remember most was that I could see down her shirt front.

I didn't mean to, no sir, not in a hundred years would I say I did. But sometimes there isn't a thing you can do but look. I saw a glimpse of her perfect body, and though she has changed some over the years, filled out, you might say, she has only become more perfect. But that sight, now that's something I never told her before. Never told anyone.

And here I am setting it down on a page with a pencil. It's time to be plain and bold and honest in all I do. Not that I haven't been a straight shooter before now. But with our Constanza expecting the first of her own babies, our very own grandbaby, why, I feel it is time for everything I know to be laid out on the table. Shouldn't take too many pages.

My wife is the one who bought me this stack of blank tablets, such as a schoolchild labors in, plus six fresh pencils, so pristine and straight and pretty in their red painted jackets, I almost did not have the heart to carve up the end of the first one. But I did, and here I am, my half-moon spectacles on the end of my nose, a tablet before me, and a cup of coffee not yet cold on the table beside my chair.

I cobbled together two pine planks and they rest on the arms of this rocker. Felice gave me scraps of flannel to tack to the underside at each end so I don't scratch the chair. And here I sit, writing down my life's story. It seems a foolish notion, as the only folks I ever heard who did such a thing were great men like

Thomas Jefferson and Abraham Lincoln and Benjamin Franklin.

But when Felice gave me the paper and pencils, she held my whiskered cheeks in her hands, looked at me, into me like only she can. That is something she has done through the years when she wants me to pay close attention. She doesn't know I do that all the time with her anyway. Her gaze pins me like a butterfly to a collector's board.

"You are a great man to me," she said.

Imagine that.

I was set to disagree, but she did something she has rarely done. Her eyes got wet and she looked away. She picked up the tablet and pencils and pushed them to my chest. "For me," she said.

And that's why I am here. Great man or no, I am not a dumb man. When a fellow like me gets lucky enough to share his life with a woman such as Felice, he does what she says. She's not steered me wrong yet.

Okay, back to it. If you've stuck with me this far, indulge me, old friend. Because the story I am going to tell you is unlike any other you will ever hear. Some of it you know, much of it you don't. It is my story, every word the truth, because I recall that summer as if it occurred yesterday.

But before I tell you about that summer, I should tell you about me, myself, and I, the only folks I ever really knew, at least up until I was almost thirteen years of age.

CHAPTER ONE

I come from a little fleabite of a town in the southwest corner of Ohio. I don't have much good to say about Duckworth, as it was called. I never learned the reasoning behind the name, odd as it is, nor do I care to know. It was a hot place in the summer and in winter it was cold enough.

Up until my eighth year, Orville Dillard Junior had a pap and a granny. My father, sounds odd to call him that, as I only ever knew him as "Pap," went by Big Dilly. I am told that from the time I appeared, I was known as Little Dilly. Pap died the year before, and then Granna, my pap's mother, up and died, too, and left me alone.

If I had known what was awaiting me, I would have hotfooted in the night for places west, north, south, or east, it wouldn't have much mattered. But I didn't know. I was young and dumb and scared. Worst of all, like my pap, I was big for my age. I might only have been nine years old, but I looked half again that. That's why the good Christian neighbor folks farmed me out. I think they were afraid they might be stuck feeding me. They said I'd be given a roof, togs, food, and schooling when possible. Ha.

My mother, Abigail MacMawe Dillard, had no say in the matter, as she perished but two, three days after pushing me out, without ever taking hold again of her senses. Granna told me all this. As fierce as she was in her devotion to her son, that'd be my pap, and to me, Granna was hard as a granite

15

boulder on the memory of my mother, or who Granna called, "that woman who birthed you."

I've studied on it a good many hours in the years that have passed, and I believe it's a simple thing. Granna disliked anything and anybody that took her son's attentions from her. If I have learned anything about people, it's that men and women love each other, and mothers often don't like it. They can be frightening in their loyalties to their offspring. I reckon in my case that fearsome attitude Granna had toward her own son naturally made its way to me.

I like to think my own mother, had she lived, would have felt that way toward me. I can only guess she must have been worked up to have to let go of me so soon. But that is a notion I kept to myself—especially around Granna. As fond as she was of me—I reckon it's because I reminded her of her own boy— she was not one to cross. I came to know what she liked and what she didn't. I learned early on not to poke her with questions about my mother.

I asked Pap about her once or twice, but it upset him so that I believed there was nobody on earth who liked the woman. Only later did I realize my pap had loved her with as much devotion as his own mother loved him. And when his wife, my mother, died, I reckon much of himself died, too. I wonder if he blamed me for thieving from him the life he could have had with my mother.

Well, all this blather won't change a thing and never will. What I was and what I am won't alter.

I was eight years of age when the very boss man himself from the freighting company where Pap worked came knocking at Granna's front door. That was the door nobody ever used, so I knew it was an important visit. It was the only time I ever saw Granna weep. But when she laid into something, she gave it her all. She kept it up for a full day and on into the night. The reason for all that tear shedding is because that man, Mr. Garbinski, I think his name was, said Pap had been laid low. I recall those were the words he used. Laid low by a rogue team.

I later overheard he got pinned between the loading dock and the rear of a wagon. He'd dropped down between the wagon and the dock to grab a sack of meal that had flopped through the gap, and he prairie-dogged up at the wrong time. Someone hadn't set the brake and the team jerked. That was when the wagon bucked backward. They say it took his head all but off.

I don't know the truth of the matter, but I do know they wouldn't let Granna see him right away, and she fought them like a cornered lion. But Garbinski and another man, who'd lingered outside our front door, held tight to her until the doctor came waddling up the steps to give her something for her nerves.

It didn't knock her out, though. I think those men were all surprised by that. But Granna was a tough old shoe, and while she did weep, she didn't lay about and moan. She cleaned the house, crying and cursing and pitching orders like there were ten of me.

It wasn't until after she'd seen Pap that she began to falter. It was no wonder, with the mess he was in. She made me peek at him, too, though that mangled man didn't much look like my pap. Folks came and went at the funeral, and Granna got old fast. By the time I gained nine years, I was tending to the house, helping her button her boots, and all but cooking each meal, too.

One morning, she didn't get out of bed, not a surprise, but the day wore on and she was still in there. I set foot in that little room that had always been hers, and where before it used to smell fresh, with something like talcum powder scented with lilac, her favorite flower, now it smelled stuffy and bad, like hair that hasn't been washed in forever, and clothes soiled from too much living and not enough fresh air.

I think I knew she was dead before I touched her hand. It was drawn up like a bird's claw, resting atop the sheet. As with Pap, Granna's face didn't much look like the woman I'd known my whole short life. She looked more like part of the blankets, wrinkling into them and away from me.

I believe I cried, though not all that much. I didn't cry again until I was farmed out, each family finding another reason to push me off on someone else.

Granna was prickly enough that once Pap died, any respect he had locally as Big Dilly, and so me as Little Dilly, was gone and forgotten. Once Granna died, I think folks wanted to rid themselves of the sad deal that was my family. Made them feel awful, I reckon. So they sent me off to work farm plots.

I'd like to say I didn't know any better, didn't hold a hard thought toward those who did this to me, but that would be a lie. And I won't tell one in these pages. I seethed inside as much as a youth can.

What I got, over and over again, was a pallet in the haymow, too-small, handed-down rags more mend than cloth, cold corn mash, colder boiled turnip, and thin-sliced meat cuts, stringy with gristle. After a time I learned not to complain, even though I knew they were eating better in the farmhouse.

As for schooling, I never did get much. One town boasted a two-room (if you count the cloakroom) schoolhouse and honest-to-god lessons four days of the week taught by Miss Horsleiffer. I saw the inside of that place but once, when the family I was hired out to, the Torbenhasts, brought me to Christmas service. That was my most memorable Christmas.

We'd got there in the sleigh, following along in a line of other such rigs, some with bells jingling about the necks of the plow horses. Of course, Mr. Torbenhast would have no truck with such foofaraw. I wondered why we were even going to the service at all. But we arrived, and I hopped down and stamped my feet and made to follow his family—Mrs. Torbenhast, and the three children, all younger than me.

Mr. Torbenhast blocked my way. I can still smell the damp wool of his coat—horse and pipe tobacco and burnt bread— Mrs. Torbenhast was always burning her bread. "Where in blazes do you expect you're going, boy?"

I knew he was talking to me, even though I'd done my level best to keep my head pulled down amongst my raggy scarf—it was only my other shirt, wrapped around my face, but I pretended it was a rich, knitted wool affair made for me and only me by a kindly aunt who was at that very minute making her way to me from her estate back East, slowed only by the cold and snow of the holiday time. But she would make it, I felt certain of it. Whoever she was, wherever she was from. The thought did its best to warm me.

I slowed my steps, and stayed in line with the others, not sniffing or coughing or letting my boots step anywhere but where they had stepped before me. That farmer moved fast, though, and I felt that big hand of his muckle down on my shoulder. I stopped.

His voice cracked close and hard beside my ear, a thick finger poking my shirt down to expose the side of my head. "You were brought here to mind the team, nothing more." He stepped past me toward the building, the windows shining like squares of sunlight, warm and friendly. His family had already gone in. He stopped, then swung his long face around. "You get cold, you can run your hands along Rock and Carl's bellies. Brush on them while you're at it." Then he made for the door.

I was left alone outside, beside the horses, a team at the far edge of a gather of them before the warm little schoolhouse. He would let me warm my hands on the bellies of the beasts. That was to be my Christmas present.

19

That and the beating.

Scarcely had he closed the door than the singing swelled up. I reckon it was because his voice was as big and loud as he was, joining the rest of the little community's members in song that night.

I left the team, stepped only where he'd stepped, and departed from the path enough to peek in a window, the closest one on the right side of the building. The gold light almost felt warm and I looked at my red hand in it. I stood on my toes and peeked inside.

The frost had melted enough that I could see in, though the shapes in there were wavy, like looking at a speckled trout holding the current in a stream. A shape moved closer, blocked the gold light, and it was Farmer Torbenhast. His eyes came clear quick enough, those great swooping brows like hawk wings jutting up.

We stared at each other a moment, then he turned away and I scampered back to the team quick, I tell you. But not quick enough. Never quick enough.

I held my breath the whole of that night, shivered my way into Christmas Day of 1892, and after I'd done my chores and most of everyone else's, too, it being Christmas morning and all, he brought me a bowl of cold corn mush and a tin cup of water, like all the normal days before it. I didn't dare look at him.

He said nothing, but stood there with the bowl. Finally, I figured he meant for me to take it from him so I reached up and he pulled it from me. I looked up. Those eyes looked the same as last night. Only now there was a mouth below them to match and it was closed tight, his jaw muscles lumped and flexing, like he had a fist on each side of his face. He shook his head slowly as if I had answered some question wrong. He snatched off my moth-gnawed felt topper and dumped the mush on my head.

It was cold and I worked my mouth like a banked fish. He tossed the tin bowl and cup to the byre floor and walked to the door.

Before he opened it, I said, "Happy Christmas, Mr. Torbenhast."

He seized in place, his hand on the handle. As soon as I said it, I knew it was the wrong thing. He'd think I was mocking him, trying to make him feel shame. It's not true, though. I was trying to apologize. He did not hear it that way.

He turned on me and I knew what was about to happen, for it had happened many times before.

The thrashing he gave me was the worst yet. And I'd learned not to try to run. I bent low and covered my face with my arms.

When he was through, I lay in the unused stall in dusty chicken dung and chaff, against the side wall where he'd pinned me. I did my best to stifle the sounds clawing their way up my throat.

"Not fit."

That's all he said. I heard his boot on the hardpan of the floor and then the stuttery sound of the door's leather-strap hinges. It squawked open, he closed it behind him, and left me to commence my sobbing, low lest he be listening outside the door, something he'd done before.

I jammed a wad of my shirt into my mouth and breathed into it. I knew I'd be sore and hardly able to move come the morning. I had much of a day ahead of me, it being early. I got moving before I stiffened. There was little for me to gather, but I took a dozen kitchen matches from the tin of them beside the lantern. Before I left the byre, I looked back and saw the dishes he'd dumped. I picked the cold corn mush out of the dunged-up muck, then slinked out the back door and into the hills where only critters who know how to survive the cold dare live.

The last thing I said as I crested the ridge behind the place was, "Happy Christmas, Dilly boy." I said it without looking back.

I'd like to say that striking off on my own was the easiest decision I ever made, and git gone to anyone blocking my path. But that is not true. Even though they were a hard lot to live with, it took more strength than I thought I had to walk away from the Torbenhast farm. How I did it, I still don't know.

Up that first hill, down its back side, and up the next. Soon enough, my feet and hands and ears—my ears started out on the large side, never did get smaller—pained me something awful, it was that cold.

I cried a streak, snotting on myself and not caring a whit. Each step brought fresh tremors of wanting to be anywhere but in that crusty snow, no decent clothes to my name. I'd even forgotten my old felt hat, even if it was filled with moth holes.

My name was hardly worth the effort it takes to spit. No one in the world cared if I was breathing air or dirt, that's a fact, yet somehow I did not give up. Though I fell a good many times, with each step I got one boot a little further than the other.

I was not worried that Mr. Torbenhast would come after me, at least not right away. I kept to myself and learned if I made no sound in the barn, he would leave me be until he needed something done. Then he would bellow. It wasn't as if I had free time. There were always more chores that needed doing—life on a farm is like digging a hole with no bottom.

Even knowing that, each step away brought worry and fear. I wanted to turn back. Only later in life have I learned why I felt that way. Here's what I came up with: When a fellow knows only one thing, even if it's the sharp sting of a knuckled hand and the cold look of one who despises you for being who you are, that fellow will still seek out that thing he knows because there is comfort in familiarity. Even if the familiar is a hard, curled thing stunted by hate and destined to keep the man from becoming what he would be were he unfettered. It takes a whole lot for a fellow to break free.

But I did not know that then. I only knew that each step took me further from the thing I hated. Long hours into my journey, it occurred to me that I had spent more time trudging toward something new than it would take me to get back to the farm. What that new thing might be, I had no idea, but the thought warmed me, though not enough. I nearly died in those hills.

I am quite certain if that blizzard had not whipped up, Mr. Torbenhast would have tracked me down. And angry as he would be, I know he would have beaten me to death in those hills and left my carcass to rot. My flesh would have fed coyotes, my bones playthings for their pups. It is a gruesome thought, and it is the truth.

But the blizzard did kick up, and though it made my life a terrifying thing for many days, it provided me with life, too, in its own fashion.

Less than an hour before dusk, the snow, which had been a pretty scene of lazy-falling flakes, became pellets that stung my face and ears. For a time I could see ten yards before me, then five, and then that pinched in half and I began slipping. I'd wrapped my spare shirt about my neck like a scarf and wrapped my hands in the ends of it, and gripped them there.

I reached the treed country of the high hills. I was between thickets, caught in an open stretch. As I angled westward, to my left, the first squall struck. That stiff, sudden gust of wind drove needles of biting ice into me.

I staggered, dropped to my left knee, my trousers already soaked through and flapping where I'd snagged them months before on a nailhead in the barn. The tear widened on a jut of snow-crusted boulder when I fell. I rested, my teeth rattling together on their own. It was no good, I had to get out of the weather.

I pushed up off the rock and made for the next cluster of trees, pines with low-hanging branches spread wide like the skirts of fancy ladies. I reckoned any tree would be better protection than standing in the clearing, crusting over with ice. The going was rough, the scree slope wanted no part in helping me get to the top in a straight line. I cut up the slope at angles, in a left-right-left-right pattern, gaining half the height with each cut. It was slower going, but got me higher quicker than if I'd struggled to carve a straight line upward.

The wind chased me up the slope, and its stinging sons and daughters, crystals of iced snow, harangued me the entire jagged route. I crawled up to the trees and I squeezed in among them to the center of the bunch. Though I wished they grew even thicker, I was grateful for any shelter at all. On top of what the winter had already brought, the snow and ice began piling up. I'd say it was a foot or more deep.

We'd had melty days back down below in the farm valley, but up high, I guessed it stayed cold all winter. I shook my head and tried to ignore thoughts of the days to come. What I needed was a fire, or I was not going to have much use for a future.

I dropped down once more on all fours, the snow cold on my hands, though they were half-numb already. I used my elbows to pull myself forward, and parted branches with my hands.

As I'd hoped, there was less snow in the space beneath the tree's bottom branches. There was even bare ground close to the trunk. I set to work building a fire, careful to position it such that it wouldn't burn down the tree, which was wishful on my part.

I tried to get that little pile of tinder to take on my first match, but I shook so that it took three before I saw the tiny, creeping glow spread into my gathered needles and bark crumbles. My shaking hand knocked it as I bent to breathe it into a proper flame. It pinched out. I have been frustrated in life, but never like that. I vowed the next match would do the trick, and it did.

The fire wasn't much to speak of, as I had very little to feed it with, but there were enough twigs and old needles around the tree's base that I was able to keep it going by offering it a tiny bit at a time. It was paltry, but offered heat if I put my big red hands over it.

The storm was a rager well into the night. I was tired and though I told myself not to sleep, I did. I had two fears, that I'd lose my fire and that I would not wake. In a spot like that, nobody except the critters would ever find me.

"Worrying about what might or might not come is a fool's errand, Dilly boy," I told myself out loud. It was something to hear my voice do more than grunt and pant. Gave me comfort to hear myself. I kept on that way, saying about anything that came to mind. And while I felt like the biggest fool alive, I wasn't going to stop.

Once the weather settled, I finally had to force myself up out of that hidey-hole. I needed more wood. The new snow made for a decent pack around me. As I climbed out, I tried to keep my tunnel small, something I could plug up again once I got back inside. I blundered about the dark thicket, and my eyes got so they could see better. The moonlight helped, reflecting its glow off the snow. The scene was so pretty I stared at it for some moments.

My teeth commenced to rattle again, and I made for the nearby trees. I snapped a fair amount of branches, half of them green. I felt badly for the trees, but cold is cold, and I was cold. I found a standing dead pine, not big around, but with some horsing I was able to snap it off below the snow, close to the ground. I broke what I could off it, carried all I'd gathered back to my spot, and went back for the rest of that tree.

I didn't think I'd be able to break much of the trunk, but I had an idea I might be able to feed it into the fire from outside, tug in a foot at a time. I did not know if it would work, but when you have nothing else, any idea sounds like it's worth your time.

I'll tell you, I kept warm the rest of that night. I had so much fire from that dead tree that I set a couple of the branches aflame above me. I reined her in. I don't believe I did that tree any good, but I like to think it recovered in a season or two.

In that way, I spent the best and worst Christmas night I ever had. I even managed to find something to eat. (I'd gobbled up the last of the dung-smelling corn mush hours before.) I had seen red squirrels work away at pine cones a number of times, and I had a supply of them under the tree. I figured squirrels are flesh and bone, same as me, so there must be something in that cone that will provide for a squirrel's crazy little body, and mine, too. It was not toothsome, as I have heard people call tasty food. In fact, it was as if I was eating wood shavings from the sawmill.

Whatever those little critters find so tasty in a pine cone must have been missing from the ones I nibbled on. I kept at it, figuring the closer to the stalk, the meatier the eating. Could be the cones I had were old and any goodness had dried up. But I do believe I felt better after I worked over three of those things. They left a god-awful taste in my mouth, with some sap sticking to my teeth for good measure. But I followed them up with a whole lot of snow, and though it made me cold inside and out once more, my gut was less grumbly.

Well, I lived through that night. Not by much, I reckon. That was the first of a handful of nights when I thought I might not wake when morning came. I got so tired I fell asleep, though. But each morning, I'd wake up.

I was young, and thick of head and muscle. After all, I'd

done the work of two men, on farm after farm, for nearly four years.

The Torbenhasts were not the first, however. They were the last. The Gileads were the first, as they'd known my Granna. Didn't mean they weren't inclined toward beatings. It's no wonder their own children left and never returned.

They were nearly as old as Granna, and while she was a tight fist of a person, the Gileads were tougher. They looked stern at me, and never smiled. Mrs. Gilead wore a black bonnet every day of the year. When she got close, usually to shout something in my face as if I was dumb, I could smell her, that greasy smell hair gets when it needs washing. He was riper, smelled of dung and old sweat. And he had two permanent tracks of chaw juice from his mouth that leaked into his chin hairs.

Also, they had a fondness for slapping and punching. I wore bruises the whole time I was with them. It is petty of me, but that's what I most recall about them, nigh on a year.

I think it might have been someone who knew my Granna who got me moved out of there, away from the Gileads. I never did find out who it was, but I was happy to be gone. Had I known what I was headed for, I would have left in the night on my own. I reckon I was young and thick of mind, and hopeful that somehow things would be better the next day. Or the next. Or the next.

I was put on a train by the same man who had brought me to the Gileads. He didn't say much, said he was from a county office of something I couldn't make out. I think someone got the wrong end of the stick about me, because once I got on board, that train kept going and going. The trip lasted a day and a night. The next morning, the porter told me my ticket was done, and unless I had more money, I had better depart from the train.

I had no money, and so I got off, a wad of clothes under my

arm and a small book of poetry by someone named John Green-leaf Whittier. I found it in Granna's room after she died. It had a brown leather covering with gold laurel leaves imprinted on it.

I never got much from the book, but having it was a comfort. It had been given to my pap by my mother, according to the inscription. It read: *To My Darling Orville. And to a future of much poetic happiness. Your loving Abigail.*

I wondered about that for some time, as it told me something of my mother, that she was a kindly soul and had once been young and happy and excited about her future, long before I came into their midst. It told me much the same about my father. And because she was not mentioned, I reckon it told me more about my Granna, too.

Why did she talk my mother down so whenever she had the chance? Why did she keep that book after Pap died? I slipped it back in my trouser pocket and stepped down out of that train onto a rough-plank platform at the depot in Chalmers, Iowa, so the painted sign told me.

As soon as I read that, I looked to my right and saw a woman in a pretty blue plaid dress standing down the platform a ways. She held her hand above her eyes and looked at where all of us passengers stood, gawking like a cluster of chickens.

I wondered if she was looking for me. And she was—marched up to me and, squinty looking, said, "You're not Orville Dillard." As if it was a fact I wasn't who I knew myself to be.

"Why yes, ma'am, as a matter of fact, I am," I said.

"You're too big."

I wanted to ask how I could be too big if I wasn't who I was. But it didn't make sense enough in my own mind, let alone trusting my mouth to make sense of it. So I did what I always did—I turned red and kept my mouth closed.

Her words stung. I have always been big for my age, and I don't need reminding of it. My feet let me know at least twice a day by catching on stumps or stones or thresholds, and pretty soon I'm fighting to stay upright, grabbing whatever's at hand and getting in trouble when I disrupt a workbench or a milk jug.

The woman shook her head and gave me the squinty eye once more before turning around. "Follow me," she said, and stomped off. I did.

Turns out her name was Jerusha Mindenhall and she'd been told to expect a small, healthy boy to help out with chores about her place as well as at the school where she taught. I was healthy, but I wasn't small. And in her eyes I wasn't much a boy any more. As chores go, there wasn't hardly enough to fill my day. She had a whole flock of ducks, about twenty of them, plus a mess of chickens and three goats. It wasn't my first encounter with goats, but it was my first time milking them.

There is a reason people should not keep goats, especially for milking. They are belligerent critters and they smell god-awful. At least the billies do.

Miss Mindenhall had two lady goats and one billy. He launched himself at me any time he thought he could get away with it. Which was pretty near all the time. I never developed a taste for goat milk, either. Too strong, it reminded me of meat gone off in the sun. It leaves a chalky feeling on my tongue that no amount of water drives away.

Well, we ended up getting along fine, me and Miss Mindenhall, for six or seven months. Then her beau, Clarence Buttersby, came out from back East, a minister in training. I tried to keep myself scarce and do what he said, but he took a dislike to me from the day he arrived at that same depot I had.

He was peevish all the time. I'd fill the woodbox and he'd tell me how I did it wrong. I'd beat the rugs and he'd stand off to the side with a handkerchief wadded in his face, shaking his head as if he'd written a book on the topic and I hadn't bothered to read it. And speaking of books, he told Miss Mindenhall that she was wasting her time, too, in what he called a "backwater town." They argued, and then they argued because they were arguing.

Soon enough, it occurred to him I was the cause of all the arguing, and he convinced her of it, too. Not long after that, the day came for me to take my leave, as she called it. It was a tearful time, as I had grown fond of Miss Mindenhall, like you do with someone you wished was your aunt. I reckon she liked me some, too. As for Buttersby, he held his kerchief to his face like he did whenever I was about, and looked annoyed with the entire situation.

As we stood on the platform, I asked her where I was being sent. "To a nice farm in Colorado. You will like it there. Plenty of children your own age, a good family, and best of all," she hugged me and said in my ear, "I have been assured they have no goats."

That made me smile. I did my best to keep that smile stuck on my face as the train departed. It lasted a whole minute or two. As we rattled away, I wondered what I had done to bring this on. I sniffed my armpits, but thanks to Miss Mindenhall, I always sported clean and mended clothes. She even bought me a decent pair of oiled boots. They weren't new, but whoever had them before me wasn't much of a walker, because the leather was still thick on the bottoms.

I left her with plenty of chores done, wood split and stacked for some weeks of use, and the coops hoed out and freshly bedded. I didn't think Clarence Buttersby would be of much use in the coops.

She had said I was headed for Colorado, which didn't matter as I had no choice in where I was going. After all, I was still not quite eleven years old. Dumb as ever, as it turns out, because I should have slipped off that train somewhere on the tracks when it slowed down, steaming and grinding up one of those long mountain passes. I should have jumped off the very end of the caboose and taken myself on down the tracks. But I didn't. And that would be one of the worst mistakes I ever made. Until that summer when the worst was yet to come.

Anyway, that's how I ended up in Clovis, Colorado, at the Torbenhast farm.

CHAPTER TWO

"Lookie here!"

I heard the voice before I saw the man it came from. The sun was in my eyes, but I squinted and leaned to my right so the gatepost blocked the sun.

Yep, there was a man on horseback, staring down at me. Still couldn't see his face, only a dark outline of a rider slouched in the saddle, tall hat with a wide brim. I'd seen plenty such hats, but for the first time in my life, I knew I was witnessing what I had heard was called a cowboy.

"I do believe I've caught sight of a weasel." He paused. "No sir, I reckon it's a polecat."

Now I knew he couldn't be talking about me. I wanted to stay hidden, but I wanted to see a polecat, whatever that was, even more than I wanted to stay hidden. I stepped out from behind the gate where I had been leaning.

The horse stepped closer, and stopped. "Nope, no, I was wrong. It's a whelp. And here I'd been picturing a platter of roasted polecat."

The man shifted. I heard the saddle make a dry, leathery sound and he blocked the sun with that immense hat. That's when I saw his eyes and a mouth smiling beneath the biggest moustaches I ever saw. When he spoke, only his bottom jaw moved.

"You got a look on your face, boy. A look I'm not certain I ever have seen."

"What?" I said, because I didn't know what he meant.

"What? What, you ask." The cowboy leaned back and the saddle made that sound again. The sun was in my eyes. I squinted. He must have seen, for he leaned forward once more and chuckled as if he'd made a joke no one else had heard. "You tell me what it is you are seeking, where you've been, where you're headed, and I'll see if this spot is the place you're meant to be about now."

I squinted again, even though he'd blocked the sun from my eyes. I was set to answer him as best as I could, though I had no notion of what he wanted, but the sound of another horse, riding up hard, interrupted our odd conversation.

"Franklin, I thought you and me are supposed to be heading to the south line, finish up that stretch of fence . . ." This second rider caught sight of me and stopped his horse. He looked me up and down. "Huh. Who's that?"

Franklin, I figured that was the first cowboy's name, said, "We were getting to that when you interrupted."

"Oh."

They both stared at me like they were waiting on me to say something. "I am Orville Dillard Junior."

Franklin smoothed out the ends of his reins. "That what people call you?"

I looked at my big feet and felt my fool ears turning red. "No, sir. They call me Dilly."

The second cowboy snorted.

Franklin kept looking at me, but said, "Shut it, Earl."

That made me feel like maybe Franklin was okay. The other one, maybe not.

"Well, Dilly," said Franklin. "I'd ask what brings you out this way, but I have been told that prodding others with questions can be taken as rudeness. So I hope you'll pardon my earlier queries."

I have met chatty fellows before, but Franklin was one for the top of the list. I reckoned that was his way of asking me without asking me where it was I was from. "I started out in Ohio." That seemed to rattle them both.

"Ohio?" said Earl. "The one back East?"

Now it was my turn to snort. How many Ohios could there be?

"Dilly, we have a pile of work to get to," said Franklin. "But the boss man, he wants to be told whenever we find somebody on the ranch who shouldn't be here. Now, out of the three of us here, that would be you. Good news is that Cook made a pile of food for breakfast and wouldn't you know, it didn't all get eaten. I figure you'd be doing him a favor if you were to deal with that while you're waiting for Boss. What do you reckon, Earl?" He faced his companion such that I could not see his expression, but I guessed what their eyes were telling.

Earl nodded. "That's about right, yeah."

Franklin rode closer.

I backed up and bumped against the gate.

"Now don't be alarmed, Dilly." He leaned down and held an arm out to me. "Grab your things and climb aboard."

"Nothing to grab," I said, aware for the first time how I must look to them. I'd caught sight of my face only the day before in a stock tank, and I'd set to washing myself with a shirt cuff dunked in the water. I'd been grimy and my hair looked like a tomcat had worked it over with its claws. But I'd managed to tame it some. I'm glad I did, else these men might not have been so inclined to take me in. Or at least, not to the cook. And while I did my best to look as if I cared not one whit about them or their boss, the promise of food was something my gut kicked up a fuss over.

"No war bag?"

I shook my head. "I got nothing else."

Again, Franklin paused and shrugged. "Okay, grab hold of my arm and I'll swing you up behind me. On three. One, two . . ."

It took two more times before I was able to take him up on his offer. It was odd, being up that high. Every time the horse took a step, I felt myself slipping, first down one side, then the other.

"You ever forked a horse before?"

That came from Earl, who was following us. I didn't dare turn to answer him. "No, sir," I said.

"It shows."

"Earl?" said Franklin.

"Yeah?"

Franklin didn't say anything.

"Oh."

In a low voice, Franklin said, "Dilly, hold onto the cantle, that's the part of the saddle betwixt you and me, or grab hold of my belt, I don't bite. Now hang on." He nudged the horse into a clunk-clunk slow run. It hurt my backside, but I didn't say anything.

We followed two wheel ruts along a lane that looked to go on straight for a ways, but it deceived me. Pretty soon we dipped down, and below us I saw four or five dark-wood buildings. Smoke rose up from chimneys on two of them. One was a long, low log affair with a wide porch along it, the other was built of planks and it also had a porch. Horses were tied out front of each.

The biggest building stood to the left, off away from the rest. It was a barn, big double doors open on one side, and a mess of horses, mostly brown and gray and black, stood inside a big wood-fenced area I knew to be called a corral.

As we clump-clopped closer, I saw people walking in and out of the buildings. Beyond them, others were riding on horses along wagon roads, brown clouds of dust puffing up behind them. But the thing I saw most of all were cows. Everywhere. More than any other critter I'd ever seen all in one place, people included. And that takes into account all those people at all the train depots I'd been through.

I must have made a sound, because Franklin said, "Quite the spread, huh? They say Mr. Hatterson, that'd be Boss, has more beeves than there are people in all of Wyoming itself."

If I knew how to whistle, I would have. I said, "Yes, sir," instead.

Franklin laughed.

We rode on up to the smaller building with the plank sides. Two cowboys were sitting outside on wooden crates, one wore spectacles pulled down on the end of his nose. They were studying over a piece of paper, but looked up as we walked over. Earl guided his horse next to us and slid down out of that saddle so quick it was almost like a conjuring trick.

"Got us a foundling," he said, stomping up the two steps toward the blackness of an open door inside.

The man wearing the spectacles took them off and squinted at me. I reckoned he should have kept them on, save himself the effort.

"Dilly," said Franklin.

"Yes?"

"Hop down so I can."

I looked around me, but it didn't seem possible. Franklin sighed and leaned forward. "Shift your weight toward me." He patted my right knee. "And swing this leg behind you. It takes some getting used to."

I managed it, but missed his left hand and fell backward from what felt like ten feet up. My backside hit first, followed by my head, which bounced. I saw the horse stomp while Franklin jumped down. "Dilly?"

I couldn't pull in air enough to fill a bean. I'd been winded before, but never this bad. A face I didn't know came close to mine.

"Boy!" He slapped my face. "Boy!" He shook my shoulder.

I sucked in a little breath.

"He's winded, is all," said the man. I knew where I'd seen him. He was the one from the porch, with the spectacles.

Franklin pulled me up by one arm, the spectacle man by the other. "Let's get on up, Dilly."

Once I was standing again, my breath came back easier. In a minute or two I was breathing okay. I was also turning so red I was beginning to purple. By that time, the porch had somehow filled with about a hundred cowboys, and one man in an apron. I noticed him because of the apron, and because he was the only black-skinned person there. Plus, he was big.

I tell you, I have felt shame a good many times, but with all those eyes on me, that day made the rest seem silly.

"Now," said the man with the spectacles. He stood in front of me, looking me up and down. "Tell me, who is this?"

Earl was leaning against a porch post. "Why, Boss, don't you know? That's what they call a foundling. They sometimes just turn up." He brayed like a donkey at his own wit. Until Franklin and the boss spoke his name at the same time.

I saw Earl scowl and push his way through the cluster of folks on the porch, and disappear inside.

"His name's Dilly, Boss."

The man with the spectacles, which were now folded in his pocket, leaned close to me. He pulled his head back quick, his nostrils flexing and eyes watering. "Does Dilly talk?"

I nodded, but said nothing. I didn't trust my breath to be there for me yet.

The boss looked up at Franklin, who was a tall fellow, now that I saw him off his horse. Franklin nodded.

"I'm still not convinced," said the boss, but he turned to face the building. "Bring him on in there, see if you can't fix him up something, okay, Cook?"

The black man on the porch was wiping his hands on a huge, grimy apron. He said, "It don't matter that I got the table cleared, no, no." He turned and walked inside. "It is a constant sound I hear, all the day long, 'Cook, do this' and 'Cook, do that.' Why, sure, Boss, I would love to interrupt my busy day to feed a flounder."

I think he meant that word Earl called me, foundling, but I wasn't about to chase after him and correct him.

Boss turned back to Franklin and, in a lowered voice, spoke past me as if I wasn't there. "While Cook heats grub for the boy, take him out back, show him our collection of lye chunks." He winked and looked at me. "Get you fed and spruced, then come on to the big house yonder. We'll talk." He nodded as if we'd come to some agreement. He turned and walked toward what he'd called the big house, which I took to be the big log house with the long, pretty porch.

As he walked past the plank shack, which I later learned was the cookshack, he said, "If that porch ain't empty quick, I expect I'll have to find me a whole new set of hands." He never shouted, but he spoke the words.

It was the second magical trick I was to see that day. The cowboys all scattered like chaff tossed in a breeze, and the porch stood empty.

Franklin guided me around the building with one hand on my shoulder. We walked up to a long, wooden trough about waist high. Franklin pointed a callused finger at a wooden bucket sitting in one end. "Water." He turned me with his big hand, and pointed at a gray rag hanging on a hook. "Towel." He turned me again and pointed at a shelf where I saw a half-dozen gray, rocky looking chunks of what I knew to be soap.

"Our lye collection."

"Thank you, but I expect I am fine," I said, straightening and turning.

Franklin turned me back toward the trough with that big hand on my shoulder. "No, Dilly. No, you're not."

"What do you mean?" I said.

"Dilly boy, you are . . . ripe."

I sniffed an armpit. I noticed there was not much shirt left there, mostly hole. "Not so bad."

"Not so good. Now strip off and wash. I'll burn those clothes of yours."

I must have looked good and frightened because he smiled. "I won't leave you naked, Dilly. There's a stack of mended togs in the bunkhouse."

He looked me up and down. "Keep your boots, though." He shook his head. "I don't believe we have anything that will fit those gunboats of yours." He winked and that took some of the sting away. I am often bothered by the size of my feet. But they keep me upright. When they aren't tripping me, that is.

It took some doing, convincing myself I needed to peel off the clothes I'd worn day and night for months. I sniffed my pits again. I don't know why Franklin was so worked up about my smell. But he seemed like a straight shooter, so I decided to take his word for it.

I shucked my top shirt—I'd given up carrying my second shirt and had for some time worn it over my other shirt. That top one came off okay. I held it up and saw through it. Like sunlight through a spiderweb. The next shirt was not nearly as pretty as the first, though for some reason it wasn't as worn through. But it was foul, I will admit that.

Around my armpits, the belly, shoulders, and the neck, heck, pretty near the whole shirt was begrimed such that I could scarcely see the blue it had been when it started out. Miss Mindenhall had given me this shirt, and I once more wished I was back there with her, tending her critters and not ever learning about her beau.

Two of the buttons fell off in my hand. I saved them in my left front trouser pocket, the only one without holes.

Under that shirt I wore my longhandles, also a gift from Miss Mindenhall. A one-piece undergarment that used to be itchy and red when it was new. But it had pinked with age and, as with the once-blue shirt, I saw this garment was more dirt than cloth.

I realized I was in a pickle. In order to take off my long-handles, I would have to peel off my trousers. I was still alone, so I got on with the job. It took me a fair bit to untie the belt I'd made for myself. It was a jag of hemp rope I sort of found on a loading dock some months before. I'd needed that very thing for some time, as I had grown tired of walking with a handful of extra cloth gathered about my waist.

I guessed my clothes had stretched with time, but I was also getting thinner the more I walked. Stands to reason, as I hadn't had a sit-down meal at a table in months. A shopkeep in a tiny town in South Dakota pitied me and gave me fishhooks and a long, thin length of twine, long enough that I could cast it a ways into water. I used that setup to land me fresh fish. I reckon that shopkeep saved my life.

It took some doing, but the knot in the rope belt loosened. I unbuttoned the front of the pants and they all but fell off me. Ended up at my ankles. I had quite a time working them over the boots. They ripped anyway when I tugged too hard.

Somewhere along my travels I lost all but two buttons off the front of my longhandles. I figured on making it a quick job and tugged that garment and found it had more holes than I needed. I ripped it as I fought to get the balled-up mess off over my boots.

I know I should have taken my boots off and gone for the full wash-down, but being all the way naked in that strange place wasn't something I was willing to do.

I got one leg off over my boot, but the second was stubborn. I wrassled it and jerked on it, all the while hopping on one foot. Up and down and around in a circle I went. I was facing the trough and my bare backside faced what I assumed was wide-open mountainside, with a passel of cows a long ways off, not interested in my efforts at cleanliness, no matter the distance.

That's when I heard it. A giggle.

A girl's giggle.

Oh no, no, no, I thought. I turned to my left, my face already redder than the noonday sun, and saw a girl watching me.

I lost my footing and fell over onto my back, all my naked-ness exposed to the air. I expect I looked like a turtle. I didn't stay that way long, though. The gravel hurt.

"Ahem," she said, turning away, but not quick enough that I didn't know she'd been staring me up and down.

I don't recall ever feeling so shamed. Why didn't I run when that Franklin first came upon me? Why did I get curious about the gate?

I knew why—I was hungry and lonely and I didn't know what else to do. My journey had not amounted to much other than to get me a long ways from where I began and I was a long ways from my last meal. The last one had been a raw fish. Maybe the last two. And that had been days before. I found roots here and there that looked and tasted something like onions, mostly alongside streams.

One time I grabbed a stick from a beaver dam. I thought I might use it as a walking stick and a spear all at once. But it was a snake and it was fast. I scared it as much as it scared me, because we both went our own way.

I lay on the ground, and with one hand clawed my raggy

shirts over to me. But I didn't dare take my eyes from that girl's back lest she sneak another look and see more of me. Not that there was much more to see.

"Are you about through?" she said. Her voice sounded high, tight, as if she might giggle again any moment.

She turned her body and faced the back of the bunkhouse, and held out a stack of what looked to be folded clothes. She waited and I waited. She realized I was not about to move from my curled-up pose, so she set them on a chopping block beside a neat couple of rows of firewood.

"Those aren't mine," I said, though it was obvious, as mine were rags all about me.

"They are now." She turned and walked away.

"Thank you, ma'am."

She waved as if swatting away my words. "Don't thank me. Thank Dunphy."

Dunphy. Okay, then.

I made certain she was truly gone from sight before I moved. I tugged up the bottom half of my longhandles and cinched the arms about my waist, safer that way, should anyone else wander on through whilst I was washing. I hurried, scrubbing on every part of me as quick as I could, dipping my sopping rag in the bucket and rubbing it on a chunk of lye soap.

Every time I finished with one hair-to-knee scrubbing, that swampy water looked blacker and blacker, so I declared myself clean and dumped the water off in some brittle weeds. There wasn't much in the way of greenery, else I would have poured it on that. On second thought, it was better I didn't. That water was foul.

The clothes were folded in a neat stack. I held them up, shook them out, and found them to be laundered, well-mended garments that replaced everything I'd taken off.

Tucked in the middle was a pair of green wool socks that

looked to be newly knitted. I sighed and eased off my boots. The stink from my big feet was considerable. I would usually tug off my boots at night, if I was camped in a spot where I felt I wouldn't get rousted in the small hours and have to leg it to safety. That happened twice, enough so that I was prone to keeping my boots on. Plus my feet didn't get so cold, and it kept the stink tamped down.

I peeled off my old socks and held them by the tops. They looked like two trouts that had been buckshot to death and left to rot. Smelled about the same, too.

I tossed them on the pile with the rest of my clothes. They would come in handy once these folks wanted their clothes back. I dragged that wrung-out rag I'd washed with all over my feet and they lightened a shade. The dirt line where I'd stopped scrubbing before was more noticeable. Looked as if I was wearing black boots.

Once washed, I pulled on the new-to-me longhandles, complete with a buttoned back door. I pulled on a shirt and tugged on the new socks. Boy, did they feel good on my sore feet. I reckon I should have carved down my toenails with a pocketknife, lest I begin a fresh set of holes in the new socks. But I had no knife. Maybe I'd buy one once I was on my own again.

The shirt's sleeves were short for me, but almost reached my wrists. I tugged on the trousers and admired the thick duck cloth. I also noted they had four buttons up the front, which meant I'd have extra work the next time I needed to pee.

The back door squawked open and the big man they called Cook stood in the doorway, wiping his hands on the dirty apron he wore. It covered a belly that on him wasn't fat so much as right. It was a slab that looked carved from wood and could take a punch without bother.

"If you're about through with primping yourself, get in here and eat before I grow so old waiting on you I give up the ghost."

He thundered back into the dark building, mumbling, and the door clunked shut behind him. I gathered my own clothes and tucked them under an arm, and I went on in. It was as dark inside as I'd guessed. My eyes took a few moments to adjust.

"No sir, no, no. You leave them rags out back for the fire. Only thing they're good for now."

"But they're my clothes."

Cook nodded. "True, but so are those." He nodded at me again.

"You mean I can keep these?"

He looked at me as if I'd asked him the quickest way to become King of China. "You think we give you those so we can see you play dress-up, like a girly's dolly?" He shook his head and walked over to the stove. "And hurry up. Cold food is wasted food, and we don't waste food here at the Hatterson Ranch."

I was back inside in seconds and saw a long, empty table. Nearly empty. At the end closest to the kitchen end of the room sat a china mug, a tin plate, and a spoon, knife, and fork. Beneath them, a folded bit of cloth.

"I don't send out invitations this time of the day. Set down, boy." Cook placed a platter of steaming flapjacks in front of the plate and plunked down a dented tin jug of milk. I could tell it was cold, as drops of dew had formed on the outside.

"Now set to it. Boy your size ought to weigh double what you do." He kept talking like that, mumbling—"Too skinny to be of use to anyone hereabouts"—slamming bowls and spoons and pans and whatnot behind me. "Eat. And when you're through, eat some more."

"Yes, sir," I said and tucked into that platter of cakes. I began with three, found that he'd set out a jar of molasses and another of berry preserves, elderberry or huckleberry, I don't know. I've never been good at telling my berries apart. Not that I cared. A berry's a berry, the sweeter the better.

From behind me I heard more clanking. "Fools, think they can go through life all skinny and useless . . ."

Soon enough I heard him clomping over to the table again and he set a big bowl of hot beans beside my elbow. "Ladle up some of those whistleberries. Flapjacks are okay, but these will stick with you. And here," with his other hand he set a plate of sizzling ham and beef hunks beside a stack of fried bread. "Don't neglect that, neither." A big finger pointed at the meat. "That will carry you when the beans wear out."

He walked to the stove and came back to the table with a tin cup of hot coffee in his hand. He sat down near me and sighed and sipped. "Boy, you best get cracking on that food. Be dinnertime before you plow through it all."

"Aren't you going to eat?"

"Me? Naw, I don't eat much." I think he almost smiled, but the cup hid his mouth. " 'Cept what I need to."

"You mean all this is for me?" I knew it was rude to ask, but I did it anyway.

He seemed amazed I would ask. He looked at the long, empty table and back to me. "You see anybody else in here?"

"No, sir." Now that I knew another six ranch hands weren't coming in for a bite of it soon, I set to all that food with vigor. I forgot to use my utensils, and only remembered when I spied the beans. They looked good, smelled better, and appeared to be made how I like them, with molasses and spices. They were dark in color, near black, and waiting for me.

"Boy, I do hope you use that spoon."

I felt my ears turn red. "Yes, sir." I picked up the spoon, and filled my mouth. The beans were better than they looked and smelled, which is saying something. That's when I noticed him watching me.

45

"Boy, you raised by wolves or baboons?"

Now my face turned red. Might have been the beans. I shook my head. "Not wolves. What's a baboon?"

He smiled, the first time I saw him do that. It made him much friendlier. I tried to keep that in mind when his eyebrows drooped again along with his big moustached mouth. "A type of monkey or some such. I thought they were wiped out of these parts, until you showed up."

I wasn't sure how to take that, figured I'd think about it later when I had the time. I picked up another piece of ham. It was sweet and salty all at once, and still warm, curling at the edges. That's when his long finger nudged the tips of the clean fork and knife beside my plate. I looked at him and his eyebrows rose and he nodded once. He looked as if he was holding his breath.

I picked up the utensils. Though I had used them in the past, it had been a while. I fumbled them for a couple of goes until I managed to carve off a ragged slice of ham and spear it with the fork. I jammed it in my mouth, and looked at Cook. He nodded and sipped his coffee.

It went like that, me eating and him watching me. You might think it was odd, being watched, but I didn't much mind. He had made the food, after all. Like a man enjoying watching a fire made with wood he's chopped himself.

I was on my last pass through the beans, and followed them with a stringy bite of beef, and sopped up the bean juice in the bowl with the last half piece of fried bread and stuffed the wad into my mouth.

"How old are you, boy?"

I opened my mouth to speak and he held up a hand. "No, no." His head shook. "Don't talk while you are eating. I've seen plenty of that food, don't need to see it in your mouth."

And so I never got to answer him, because he slid the wiped, empty dishes from before me. "This here ain't normal, mind you. Don't you ever let me catch you saying how I cleared your place." He nodded and walked heavy-footed back to the kitchen.

"Yes, sir." I wasn't certain what I should do next, so I carried the preserves and milk jug back to the kitchen. They were a fair bit lighter than when he'd set them before me.

"There." He nodded toward a cluttered wooden shelf beside the stove. "Good. Now, you got somewhere to be, or are you a loafer?"

"No, sir. I mean, yes, I think I'm supposed to go to that other house."

"You think? Didn't Boss tell you to?"

"Yes, sir."

"Well, that's your answer. Ain't no thinking about it."

"Yes, sir." I made it to the table. "Thank you for the breakfast. That's about the best food I ever ate." I meant it, too.

Cook was silent for a moment, one of his big hands resting on the handle to the stove door. "Okay, then. Best get to it."

As I walked out the door, I heard him say, "Near big as a man, yet he can't be but a child. Grown folk ain't got the strength to hide away that much food."

I walked to the big house wondering about Cook. I was not certain if I'd riled him or if he was naturally surly. I didn't act any different than I usually do around folks I only just met. It's not like what he thought of me would matter. I'd be gone soon enough, and he could get back to whatever he was doing before I annoyed him.

CHAPTER THREE

I climbed the steps of the long porch and was about to knock on the door when it opened. There stood that girl who'd seen me near-naked. I reddened to the top of my hair again. She smiled and that made it worse. I didn't get much of a look at her before, as I was busy trying to hide myself from her, but now that I saw her, she was some pretty.

"Come on in," she said. "I expect you're here to see the boss."

I nodded, but I could not look her in the eye.

"Those clothes fit you," she said, half turning as we walked down a hallway.

"Yes," I said, finally. "Thank you." My voice wasn't much more than a squeak. I was going to repeat myself when she knocked once on a carved door, and swung it open.

There was Boss, looking the same as he had outside, except his big hat hung on a peg on the wall near his desk, which he sat behind. The desk was like the hat: big. Maybe that's because Boss wasn't a very big man. Oh, he was full grown, but not tall. More like a chunk of firewood, all solid but not quite a tree.

Must be something to the fact that men that size always surround themselves with big things. Like hats and desks and horses and ideas and attitudes. I met a number of such men on my travels, and they usually wanted me to know they were the boss of this or that. I didn't much care, but if there was a meal or a chance of working for a meal, I'd listen to them go on and on all day. I hoped Boss wasn't like that. It gets tiresome.

I gave the room a quick look-see. The walls looked to be built of books.

"Thank you, dear." Boss smiled at the girl and she left us alone. "Have a seat . . . Dilly, you said?"

I nodded and sat in the chair in front of his desk. It was wooden, but the seat and back were cow hair, almost like they'd taken a cow and folded it up into a chair shape. It was more comfortable than a rock, but not by much. I didn't say anything about it.

"What brings you to the Hatterson Ranch, son?"

Boss leaned back and hoisted one boot up onto an open drawer beside him back there behind the desk. He packed a pipe and fiddled with it forever. I didn't much mind as I love the smell of pipe tobacco. Almost as much as I love the smell of fresh baked biscuits. As if he was reading my mind, Boss said, "I hope Cook fed you up in good shape."

"Yes, sir. He did."

I almost told him how much I ate, only because it was of such an amount, I was impressed with it myself. But I kept my mouth shut, as it occurred to me he was the one who paid for that food. I figured I ought to answer his first question, but I didn't want to interrupt him.

He set fire to the pipe's bowl and drew on it, two, three times, then pushed out a big blue cloud that took its time rising up away from his head. It held there a while and broke apart. "I like a pipe after a meal. My Myra says it's a foul habit."

"Is that your wife, sir?" I surprised myself with that. I was nervous, and didn't know what to say.

He shook his head. "No, my daughter. You met her." He smiled and winked.

Sure enough, I turned red. Had to be the girl who'd seen me in my nakedness. Except for my boots. From his wink, I bet she told him all about it. Sooner I could git gone, the better I'd feel about the whole day. But I had to stay for a spell. They did feed me and clothe me, after all.

"I'd like to thank that Dunphy fellow who gave me these clothes."

Boss leaned back in that chair. It made that leathery, wood squawk again. "Dilly, are you a praying man?"

I don't mind admitting I liked being called a man. I may have puffed up. I leaned back in my chair, too, and held my knee in my hands, like I've seen sitting men do. "I . . . I guess so." In truth, prayer was not something I'd given much thought. "Why?"

"Because the only way you're going to converse with Reginald Dunphy is if you have a direct trail to the Almighty."

I must have looked like a dog that hears a noise he's not heard before, because Boss said, "He's with the angels, Dilly. Dunphy's dead. Horse rolled on him oh, six, eight months back. He had no kin that we knowed of, but he was a tidy man, kept his traps clean."

I looked down at my new clothes, all manner of horrible thoughts bubbling through my head. Boss's laughter made me look up.

"Dilly, son, you should see your face. Those aren't the clothes he died in! We buried him in those. Roundup was on, no time for frivolities. Oh, we gave him a decent send-off, read over him. And a month or more ago the boys carved him a fine marker. Those clothes there," he pointed his pipe stem at me, "they're his spares. Good fit for you, though."

I was relieved, even though I was wearing a dead man's clothes. Another thing I'd have to think about later when I had the time.

I stared around the room while Boss stared at me. That was something about this ranch, everybody seemed to be watching me. Out front of the bunkhouse, the girl while I was washing,

Cook while I ate, and now Boss. Oh well, they fed me and clothed me. Let them stare. I wasn't about to do any tricks.

I'd seen books, of course, even knew how to read, and did so in my own book, at least until Mr. Torbenhast took it from me, tore it apart like it was no better than a page from the Roebucks catalog in the privy. Few things have been done to me that I can't work through and forgive, except that. If that makes me less of a fellow than I could be, I do not care. A book is a special thing.

"How old are you, Dilly?"

I cleared my throat and sat up straight. "I am almost thirteen, sir."

Boss's mouth sagged open and his pipe wagged downward. He caught it before it fell out of his mouth, and leaned forward, elbows on the desktop. His reaction didn't much surprise me. I have grown used to people being surprised when they learn I am not as old as my size hints at.

"Are you certain, Dilly?"

At that I almost laughed. I might not have had a whole lot, but I had my mind, and I knew my birthday, even celebrated it in my head those past few years of moving from one place to another. I nodded. "Yes sir, I am positive of it."

He leaned back in his chair and puffed up another cloud. "Sometime we should have a chat about our families, where we come from, all that. I am fascinated by what brings people out this way."

I could tell he wanted to know more about me. I didn't see any harm in telling him about myself. "I am from Ohio."

"The state of Ohio?" he said, sounding like Earl had.

"Yes, sir."

"Did you take a train or a stage to get out here?"

"Well sir, I rode a train to Iowa a year or so back, and another to Colorado. From there I mostly walked. Sometimes I got a ride on a wagon. Hopped on a boxcar one other time. Helped out with some freighters a few months back, but they traveled southwestward and I had it in mind to move north, so I kept going."

"I see." He wasn't puffing on his pipe anymore. "Are you looking for anyone? Anything in particular?"

"No, sir," I said. "Just walking."

"Ah. Well, have you ever worked on a ranch?"

"I have worked on farms, tended all manner of critters. Chickens, horses, a fair number of cows, goats and sheep, too."

At that, Boss's eyes narrowed. "Well, there are no sheep on the Hatterson. A fouler beast you'll not find on God's earth." He pulled in a deep breath and didn't talk for a few moments. I wasn't certain what I'd said to rile him, but it was looking like this place was full of folks to walk tender around.

He set the pipe in a bowl on his desk, and he smiled again. "How did you get along with Cook?"

Now there was a tricky question. I liked the meal, and I did my best to be pleasant with the big man, but I wouldn't call it getting along with him. "Fine, sir. He's a good . . . cook."

Boss nodded. "We're lucky to have him. But don't tell him I said that. The old bear will want more money from me."

I smiled.

"So how would you like to work for him? Well, you'd be working for me, but you'd answer to him. He could use help with the firewood, and everything else he does. Lord knows there aren't enough hours in the day for any of us to do all that needs doing around here. And with the blasted sheepmen moving in, there's more fence than ever to build."

"Me, work for Cook?"

"Yes, why, would that be a problem for you?"

"No sir, but . . ."

"But what, Dilly?"

52

I decided to come out with it. "Well, I'm not so sure he likes me all that much. He wanted to know if I was raised by a baboon."

Boss chuckled. "Sounds like Cook. That's a new one, though. Don't take it personal. A few weeks back he called me a, oh, what was that word?" He leaned back, then shot forward again, his boots clunking the floor. He snapped a finger and smiled. "A Neanderthal. You know what that is, Dilly?"

I shook my head, but figured as ornery as Cook was, it had to be a pretty bad word, though why someone would call their boss a bad name was a question I could not answer.

"Well, look it up some time. That's what Cook does. I myself like a book now and again, but that man, oh, he's a reader. He'll borrow one of these books and read it five, six times through. Practically knows 'em word for word by the time he's done. He never forgets a thing in them. Now you take your pal, Franklin. He reads books like most men breathe. But he's not only a reader, he's a genuine learned man. Educated at an eastern land grant college and all." He nodded as if it was something he himself had accomplished. Maybe he had.

I wondered why he would call Franklin a learned man when he owned so many books himself.

We went on like that for a spell, then Boss slapped his hands on his desk. "Time to quit jawing away the day. I have things to do." He snatched his hat off its peg and walked to the door, holding it open for me. "And so do you. Tell Cook I said you'll be working for him and not to go easy on you. Don't want any soft hands on the Hatterson Ranch."

We'd made it outside and down the porch steps, and that was it. Boss vanished on his horse in a boil of dust and I walked back to Cook's kitchen.

I told Cook what Boss had said about me working for him, but I didn't say anything about Cook not going easy on me. I bet myself all the money I didn't have that Cook was going to keep me busy. And I was right. Not a minute after I told him and he mumbled something about having to be stuck with a flounder, I was out back again, working a bucksaw on a pile of pine logs that looked as big as a house.

"Make 'em no longer than stove length, now, or you'll be cutting them down again. And when you work your way through that pile, start splitting them. That should keep you until dinner. Then wash up, 'cause you're going to help me serve the men."

I stared at him a moment too long, because his eyebrows rose up like big woolly worms. "I will give you five seconds, then I don't want to see nothing but your backside and them elbows working that saw. You understand me, Dilly boy?"

"Yes, sir." And I set to work.

CHAPTER FOUR

I would like to say that my first day at the Hatterson Ranch was filled with excitement and guns and horses, but most of what I remember is making stovewood out of logs and getting blisters for my efforts.

Cook made it plain with me that there was no way, no how, a person could expect to serve food in his kitchen, food that he worked all day to prepare, and do it with grime on his hands. Same goes for eating. I washed.

He said that me and him would eat before the men came in. We did so at the same end of the table, in the same spots where I ate breakfast and he watched me. But with plenty of time to spare so I could clean off the table, wash those soiled dishes, and set the entire rest of the table. I thought cutting firewood was hard, but Cook knows how to keep a body moving.

I got a few long looks by the ranch hands when they tramped in from washing their hands and faces. I recognized half of the men from seeing them stare at me that morning. The only one I knew by name was Earl. Franklin was not yet there, but that Earl, he stood behind his spot on the bench, and looked me up and down longer than he needed to. He narrowed his eyes and shook his head as if to dispel an irksome fly.

"If that don't beat all," he said. "A whelp wanders in off the trail looking for free food, and he ends up serving us our food! Careful, boys, else that big-footed stompin' baby will have himself a feast from your very own plates!"

"Earl."

The chuckling men looked up to see Franklin standing in the doorway, drying his hands on a scrap of towel.

It made me feel good to see him. Now that I was clear-eyed and wasn't lying on my back out front, addled in the dust, I saw Franklin as even taller than I recalled from the morning.

He sat down in the middle of all those men packed tight on the long benches. There were two chairs, one at each end. An older fellow whose hand shook as he sipped a cup of coffee sat at the far end of the table. And that was coffee I poured, I don't mind saying.

As Cook showed me, I walked around the table, to see if each man wanted coffee. Cook said I should hold out the pot, and only if the man didn't first show me with a nod or a finger motion that they wanted coffee was I to open my mouth and ask. They all nodded or held up a finger.

My job was to lay out the platters of food—slabs of steaks, all fried up, as Cook said, "until they're good and dead. No sense risking it." What "it" was, I don't know. But that meat was some cooked, blacker than I'd fry it. But what did I know about it? As Cook said, I haven't been eating as long as he has.

Once all the food was laid out, it was my job to make certain none of the platters of meat or biscuits or bowls of beans or jugs of milk and water or cups of coffee ever went empty or dry. I was supposed to reach between the men, pick it up, unless they handed it to me, and get it on out of there. He had me dump whatever was left on that bowl or platter onto a fresh one and bring it back to the table quick. It looked to be a whole lot easier than chopping wood. Or so I thought when Cook first explained it to me.

I got around to Franklin at one point, and leaned in to pick up a plate that had but one biscuit left on it. I knew there were fresh ones just baked, so I wanted to get them on over there. I said, "Hi Franklin, I want to thank . . ." when he said, "Hush now, Dilly," without even looking at me.

My ears bloomed red and I made quick work of bringing biscuits back to the table. I understood what I'd done wrong without having to ask. There was no sound in the room save for men sawing meat, chewing, belching, sniffing, snorting, or farting. The only thing I didn't hear were words. Talking at Cook's table was not tolerated.

After a half an hour or so, the men cleared out as fast as they had come in. The only sounds were benches squawking backward, and groans, and hands slapping full bellies as they walked out to the porch. I set to clearing the table, hoping Cook was impressed with my efforts. I tried to remember what he'd told me, which wasn't all that much to begin with. I was learning I had to translate his grunts and nods into tasks.

I carried a stack of tin plates—most of them licked clean—over to him, but he shook his head and nodded toward the back door. I understood. I was to wash them in the same trough where I'd washed myself that morning.

I walked back inside from stacking the plates in the washing-up trough. Cook was at the table, wiping the plank top with a sloppy wet rag. "You did a fair job with serving, Dilly." He said it without looking up.

"Thank you."

"But," he straightened and looked down at me, one thick finger wagging, the sopping rag dripping on the floor beneath it. "I guess by now you know we do not talk at my table."

"Yes, sir. I figured that out."

"I know you did." He turned back to washing the table. "Good. When you finish washing those dishes, come on inside and help me get set up for the morning. It comes quick."

"Yes, sir."

"If there's time, we'll go set out on the porch with the other men and discuss the day, maybe listen to Hector and James lie to each other. And Pedro usually has his mouth organ. We're lucky, he might give us a tune. You like music?"

He didn't wait for me to answer.

"I always wanted to play piano, myself, but these fingers are so thick I am afraid it would sound like rocks falling on the keys."

I wanted to laugh but I didn't dare. I made for the dishes and let the door slam behind me.

"Dilly boy . . ." He followed me out. "That door was not made to be slammed. Except by me." He mumbled as he walked over to the trough. "You see that bristle brush there? We use that to scrub on the plates. The bean pot don't hardly ever get scrubbed because I keep adding to it. I make beans every day of the week. Besides, an old ship's cook taught me once that a good chef never cleans the pots and pans he uses most. You wipe 'em down with a rag. You go scrubbing on them, they'll lose all their seasoning. Takes years to build that up. Food won't taste right."

He leaned in and pointed a big finger in my face. "So don't let me catch you scrubbin' on anything you ain't supposed to, you hear?"

I nodded, wondering what I was supposed to scrub and what I wasn't.

He gave me a quick lesson in how to scrub the plates, the utensils, and platters, and left me to it, mumbling as he walked back into what I learned was called the cookshack. The door didn't bang too much. Even if it had, I wasn't about to say a thing.

I scrubbed everything twice, in case, even though I wanted to get out to the porch to see what the ranch hands got up to after they ate. It could be fun to listen to them swap lies and hear a tune. It had been a long time since I heard music. Well, music made by anyone but myself. I am not much for singing, but I will hum once in a while, and I do like to whistle.

I like to imitate the birds I hear as I walk. They are the best musicians I have ever heard. Could be that I haven't heard enough music to know better. But the birds are so pretty to listen to sometimes. Except for crows. They sound like a crosscut saw slicing through knotty wood.

Must be all the fun was had before I got out there, or the hands decided it was going to be a quiet night.

Cook was already out there. He'd shucked his big apron. His hands were folded on his belly, and he had one big leg flopped over the other.

There was plenty of space next to Franklin, so I sat down beside him.

He nodded. "Dilly."

So I did the same. "Franklin."

Out before us the night was purple, lighter up toward the sky and darker where it met the land. I decided this might be the prettiest time of the day.

Other men were chatting low with each other, so I wiped my nose with my arm and said, "I meant to ask Cook earlier, how come there was an empty seat at the far end of the table?"

Franklin stretched his legs and wiggled his toes. I would come to learn he'd take his boots and socks off to let his "feet breathe." He said and did odd things like that, things I had never heard other folks say.

"Sometimes Boss likes to join us for grub, if he can talk Myra out of cooking for him, which isn't too often." He leaned closer and spoke low, his voice a rumble, "Nice girl, but cooking doesn't seem to be one of those skills she inherited."

"Ah," I said, as if I knew what he was talking about. I'd think on it later. "I reckon she cooked tonight," I said.

"Well," said Franklin. "I expect it was cattle business. You might have been too busy chewing away at that log pile out back to notice Boss had company this afternoon. A couple of local ranchers like himself. I expect they were talking about the sheepmen."

"What are sheepmen?"

Franklin smiled. "Not as exotic as it sounds, Dilly. They're people who ranch sheep same as we ranch here with cattle. Got a pile of them hereabouts."

"There's a whole lot more difference than that," said Earl from the dark, down the porch a ways. "We all know them muttonheads ain't all human. What they need is a good ol' disease. That'd take care of them."

"Don't you listen to him, Dilly," said Franklin. "Sheepmen have as much right to be here as cattlemen."

"You ought not to fill the boy's head with such notions, Franklin. He's already addled enough from his tumble off your horse this morning." Earl laughed and so did a couple other fellows. I was glad it was dark out there, else they would have seen my ears turn red.

"You going to take that from him?" said Franklin in a low voice that I bet only I heard.

I shrugged, didn't look up.

"No worse than that dive you took two days ago on the high trail, eh, Earl?"

I knew Franklin was trying to make me feel better. I appreciated it, as I never did know how to talk with folks like Earl. All they want to do is cut you down. I try my best to stay away from folks like that in life, but it doesn't always work.

"Aw, Franklin, you know that roan was spooked by a rattler. It crow-hopped on me, was all I could do to hold on. I'd like to have seen you do any better."

Franklin chuckled and wiggled his toes. "I don't recall any rattler in attendance, but now that you mention it, I do remember that horse dancing on you. It was cute, almost like a parade mount." That brought out a few laughs.

I was surprised Cook wasn't saying anything. I watched as his foot draped over his other leg, bouncing to a tune only he heard. I hoped Pedro would take that as a cue to pull out his harmonica, but there was no sound other than a night bird, what sort, I don't know.

Sometimes I heard a match when one of the hands lit a cigarette or a pipe.

Sudden cries bloomed from out of the dark. It took me a moment to remember it was coyotes. They commenced to yip-ping from what sounded like two or three directions all at once. They stopped as quick as they all started, and it was quiet again. Except I began to hear yawns pretty regular.

Setting like that is the last I recall until Franklin woke me. Or more to the point, it was his finger that did, prodding into my arm. I'd dozed on the bench.

"Dilly. Hey, Dilly. Time to crawl into your soogan, boy. Tomorrow will be here quicker than yesterday. I'm due for the sleep sack myself. It's been a long day." He stood and stretched. "I expect you feel the same. I hear Cook's been keeping you hopping like a frog on a hot skillet."

I stood and noticed the porch was mostly empty. Cook was sitting by the door with his arms folded, staring down the porch at me. There were a few dark shapes walking off toward the bunkhouse.

I had not thought of where I was to sleep. I assumed it was the bunkhouse, but when I reached the top step, Cook said, "Uh-uh, Dilly. This way."

He held the door to the cookshack open and I walked back in. I wondered if I was ever going to see any more of the place.

"You'll be nesting down that end." He pointed toward the kitchen. "That's where I stay. Got a bunk off to the side set up for you. Been a while since I had help, so I was using it to hold sacks of beans. Our day starts earlier than anybody else's, so it makes sense for us to be close by the kitchen."

"Yes, sir," I said, feeling a sudden wave of sleep wash over me. He could have been telling me he sprouted feathers and I would have said, "Yes, sir."

All I remember is flopping down on that bunk, and I think Cook was chuckling as he pulled a wool blanket over me. Might be I dreamed it, I don't know. And that put an end to my first day at the Hatterson Ranch.

If I had known what life there would lead to, I don't know as I would have stayed on. But that's the funny thing about life, you can't tell what's coming next.

CHAPTER FIVE

The next day began as a hot one. And after breakfast there I was, whacking away at that pile of wood. First I'd take time with the bucksaw, then I'd give that a rest and go at the logs with the axe. I find that chunking a task into smaller bits makes the work less boring, and cutting wood can be tiresome.

I'd been giving it good licks when I noticed the banging and clanking from the kitchen stopped. I stopped, too, figuring it was time for a drink of cool, clear water.

I was drying my neck with my shirt when Cook pushed open the door. "This here part of the day is your time to do what you want. A man can't work all day, every day, Dilly. That makes for a dull life and a quick one. Best you learn that now while you're still a pup. You know how to read?"

"Yes, sir."

"I figured you for a readin' man. Good. If you like, you can go to the big house, borrow books. Franklin does, so do I." He puffed up at that.

I pulled on my shirt, buttoned up quick, and jammed the tails into my trousers. I didn't want to waste any of my free time. I didn't know exactly what it meant or how long it would last, but I liked the idea. Like finding a coin in the dirt, so full of promise, you know it will bring something good, even if you don't know what that might be yet. "Maybe I'll ask about a book."

He pointed a big, dripping wooden spoon at me. "You mind

you knock on that door, and ask nice and polite."

"Yes, sir." I made for the far end of the building and turned. "You want me to bring you back a book, too?"

"Me? No, I'm still chewing on a novel by Mr. Charles Dickens. I don't know what to think of him yet. Expectations shouldn't be great, they should be humble. Unless you work hard. Seems to me those people in his book are expecting way too much for the efforts they put in."

"Yes, sir," I said, but I do not know what he was on about.

"You make sure to knock and ask if it is a convenient time to borrow a book. If it ain't, Boss or his daughter will tell you to come back later. You hear me?"

"Yes, sir."

"Okay, then. Get on with it."

I was tempted to go to the big house to borrow one of those books, but I was so new to the Hatterson, I figured first I'd take a walk around the ranch yard proper. I'd not seen all the buildings yet. I should know the lay of the place if I was going to live and work there. I walked past the bunkhouse when I heard scuffling noises from around the other side of the barn. I remembered that's where the corral was, so I made for it.

I saw Franklin walking a horse around and around inside the corral. The horse wasn't saddled, but had a bridle on and he led it with about a ten-foot rope, talking low and making clucking, soothing noises. The horse appeared to limp a little but walked with weight on all its legs. I know a little about horses, from my time around them on farms, harnessing them and hooking them to wagons or buggies or plows.

I climbed up on the rails and hung my arms over the top and watched them. When he made a new pass, Franklin saw me watching. "Well, hey there, Dilly. You out carousing?"

I shrugged. "I reckon." Though I didn't think I was.

He laughed and walked over with the horse. It stood close by him and rested its big head on his shoulder, its rubbery nose working for something. "You're a hog, not a horse," said Franklin, but he was smiling.

As he pulled out a slice of dried apple from his shirt pocket and fed it to the horse, he said, "Dilly, meet Montgomery. Montgomery? Dilly."

"How do you do, Montgomery?" I said, nodding my head and trying to sound important.

Franklin pulled a serious look on his face. "You don't really think horses can speak English, do you, Dilly?"

I turned red, and he chuckled. "I'm joshing you. No, old Monty here has been around the ranch for quite a spell. He still has a few good years in him, but he's got a chilblain on his leg that acts up now and again. I exercise him out here when I get the chance. He's a lot like most of us, Dilly. If left to his own devices, he would stand in his stall and do nothing. The best thing he can do is move his body, keep these big legs of his limber."

"So you help him do that?" I said, stroking Montgomery's long nose.

"Yep, I do. But not enough. There's more blasted fence to build every day. Say, you wouldn't want to give ol' Monty a few turns around the corral every now and again when I can't, would you, Dilly?"

"I could do that," I said, though I was a little afraid because Montgomery was such a big horse. Funny I should feel that way, as I'd rigged up draft horses for years and wasn't much afraid of them. But Monty was different. He was a genuine cowboy horse.

"I bet you even know where to get fruit for him. He likes carrots, too, though I can't imagine Cook would be pleased to find out his carrot supply was disappearing down the gullet of ol' Montgomery. Best stick to a few slices of dried apple."

I nodded, smiling. Something I'd been wondering about came to my mind. "Hey, Franklin?"

"Yes, Dilly." He'd begun walking around the corral again. I followed, scuffing along outside the rails.

"Last night you said you don't hold with how they're treating the sheepmen, but you go along with it, and keep working here."

Franklin nodded, not looking at me as he clucked to the horse. "Yep, I ride for the brand."

"What's that mean?"

Franklin regarded me as if I'd broke wind at the dinner table. "Think about it, Dilly."

I nodded, still unsure of what it was I was supposed to think on. I'd get it, I don't like to give up on a thing. A few minutes of silence passed, then I said, "Does it mean if you take a man's money, you don't have a right to think for yourself?"

Franklin's eyebrows rose under the broad brim of his fawn-colored hat. "Well now, that's a hard way of putting it, but yes, there is something in what you're saying. I'd be more inclined to say that if you work for a man, you are obliged to do his bidding, even if some of what he asks you to do might rub you the wrong way."

"I see," I said, and I think I did understand what he was getting at. "So you don't mind the sheepmen."

"They don't bother me much, no."

"But they bother Boss."

"That they do."

"From what I've heard, those sheep are eating all the grass on the boss's land. Seems like he has a right to be bothered."

"You're correct in saying the sheep are eating a whole lot of acreage down to the nub. Sheep will do that, whereas cows will leave more of the stem to grow, not so greedy a creature. But you're wrong in saying it's all the boss's land."

He rubbed Monty's long nose. "Boss only owns two sections.

The rest of the land you see, and most of it you don't, over there," he jerked his chin toward the north, the closest range of mountains, low hills really, behind the place. "And there, and there, all around us, really, it's most all open range, public land, anyone can graze their critters on it. It doesn't belong to anybody in particular."

"Why don't they share it?"

Franklin tapped his nose with a long finger. "You smacked that nail on the head. That's a good question, Dilly. The cattlemen like Boss and Delahanty and Chase, they've been here a long time. Some of them were the first white men to settle in the area. They did a whole lot to keep the tribes from overrunning it, opened it up for folks who came later. Those are the ones who settled towns like Greenhaven. Brought the stagecoach line, farmers came in, and trains. So the ranchers feel like they've earned the right to keep this land for themselves."

"That's why they're fencing it off?"

"Yep. And between you and me, putting up fences isn't exactly legal. But they figure once they do it, it will become acceptable and folks will get used to it."

That didn't make a lot of sense, but I knew it was something I could chew on while I sawed wood. I hopped down from the corral rail.

"Dilly, just because you ride for the brand doesn't mean you can't be your own man."

I nodded, but was not so certain it made sense. It sounded like he was saying that to make himself feel better about doing something he didn't really believe in.

"I best get back, Franklin."

He nodded. "Okay. But don't forget, Monty likes his apple slices."

"Yes, sir."

CHAPTER SIX

It must have been my second week at the Hatterson Ranch when Cook came up behind me while I was working that bucksaw for all I was worth.

"I almost hate to interrupt you, Dilly, but there is something that needs cutting even more than that wood."

Whatever it was, I was game to give it a go. I'd not yet worked up a sweat, so I wasn't too bothered. I normally don't like to stop a task when I'm in the middle of it. I leaned the saw on the little pile of lengths I'd cut and pushed my hair out of my face.

Cook said, "We're going to shear us a boy-size sheep." He grinned and held up shears, a smaller set than those we'd used to trim the wool off the sheep come springtime. I didn't say anything about that, though. I'm not certain how Cook feels about sheep, likely the same as Boss. It occurred to me I was the sheep he was about to come at with those cutters. I backed up.

"You look like you been living with heathens, boy. I can't have someone looks like you serving food at my table."

"What's wrong with the way I look?" I shoved that blasted hair away from my eyes again.

"There now! You see?"

I shook my head.

"That's what I'm talking about. You didn't have all that hair hanging in your face, you'd see what I was on about."

I admit that my hair had been a bother to me for a while.

The last time it was trimmed, I did it. But it was cold, so I only cut the front so it wouldn't hang in my eyes. I got a look at myself in a stream afterward and decided I looked foolish, so I vowed to leave it be.

Well, it was in my eyes again, had been for some time. If I had a hat it would not be so bad, as I could tuck the entire affair up under there and leave it alone. But I did not have a hat. I never asked about wages, but I reckoned Boss or Cook would pay me something at some point and I would be able to buy a hat for myself. I fancied a big, broad-brim cowboy style that curved down in the front and only had a little curl on the sides, enough brim to keep the rain and sun off.

As to my hair, it is curly and red and thick, like grass clumps or knots of wire. When I was a child, sometimes Granna would take me to town to do her shopping. Women were forever touching my hair and fussing over it. You'd think that might tug up a smile on Granna's face, but nothing really did.

As soon as I was old enough to stay alone and get up to some work without needing her telling me what to do, she left me at home while she did the monthly shop. Or as she called it, "visiting the thieves." She claimed shopkeeps were forever stealing from her coin purse, which I never understood, as she kept it tied tight and double-knotted on a cord about her neck. She held merchants in lower regard than about anyone, save for what she called the "blue-devil sinners." I still don't know what they are.

Something about the way Cook come at me with those scissors set the creeping willies dancing up and down my backbone. I stepped to the side, ready to dash away.

His eyes got squintier. "Now boy, you want to keep working here, we got to tend to that mess of snakes sprouted all over your head. Why, I can't expect the men to eat food your hair's been hanging all over, can I? Bad enough you don't bathe regular then."

"My hair is fine, Cook. As soon as I save up, I'm going to buy a hat and there won't be a problem."

"What you going to do at mealtime, huh?" He stepped closer.

I hadn't thought of that. Cook didn't allow hats to be worn at the table.

"Besides, way you eat it's going to be a long time before you can buy yourself a hat. And by then, we'd all be choking on your hair." He chuckled and set a hand on my shoulder. I knew I'd lost. "Look at it this way, Dilly. I'm about to save you the price of a new hat."

He had me sit on the chopping block. I got to thinking about all the chickens who ended their days there, having something done to their heads, too, and by somebody holding something sharp. Likely the same fellow.

I tensed and Cook plopped a bowl on my head, upside down.

"What's that for?"

"That's for cutting your hair even across the front. Rest of it I'll take a stab at."

I tensed again.

He sighed. "I meant to say I will do it without the bowl, that's all."

Cook snipped on my head awhile, slow and mumbling the whole time. I only heard a word now and again, something about a rat nest. As he promised, he gave up on the bowl and went at it with nothing but his eyes and those shears, which looked bigger and sharper than before. He also bit the end of his tongue a lot. I believe it helped his concentration, so I didn't say anything. But I wanted to. Cook finally spoke.

"Considering what a chore it has been to get you to sit here, I'm cutting it short so we won't have to go through this any time soon. But I am leaving enough so the women will like it." He winked.

I felt my ears heat up.

"Lordy, boy, you got enough lumpy scars, your head looks like an explorer's map. What you been up to? Butting heads with one of Boss's barbwire fences?"

I tried to laugh. I didn't want him to feel bad, but I felt my ears go red again. I wished I could cure those things.

"Ain't no shame in things you been through, son. All that matters is if you get up to mischief or good things today and again tomorrow. You tell yourself that each day, 'cause each new day that comes is today. And the next day will always be tomorrow, you hear?"

"Yes, sir." And I did. I felt sure there was something important in what he was telling me, so I vowed to think on it later while I was chopping kindling.

He ran his big fingers over my head again. "Hmm, you better hope when you get to be an old man you don't go bald, 'cause you'll be a sight." Cook chuckled. "Marry a blind woman and you'll be all set."

I laughed.

He clipped some more and hummed a little, too. It was nice. I was about to join in when he said, "You ain't shaving yet. But you might want to consider it. Leastwise nub off those odd hairs on your chin and cheeks. Looks like you have bugs crawling on your face."

I wondered if that's what people thought of when they looked at me. The idea bothered me.

"Cook?"

"Yep."

"Say I wanted to grow a moustache, oh, like Franklin's, for instance." I glanced at him, but it looked like he was busy chewing on his own moustache, or maybe he was going to sneeze. I couldn't be certain.

"Well," he said finally. "Now, Dilly, that's an admirable goal.

71

But you have to understand it's going to take a good long while before it looks like that."

"How long?"

"Oh, a while."

"Years' worth?"

"Mm-hmm, could be."

"Oh." I was not impressed with this news.

"Hold your head up, boy. Don't go all hangdog on me."

"Yes, sir."

"You want to know a secret, though?" Cook leaned close to me. "The more you shave, the thicker it grows."

I looked at him to see if he was funning me.

He nodded. "Shave off that baby hair and soon enough it's the real thing. It's true. I ain't never lied to a man in my life and I'm not about to begin. Especially to a kitchen whelp. Now sit up straight. I'm not through yet."

Cook kept on snipping, and said, "I can see there's something else on your mind, Dilly."

"Well, it's about hair."

"Mm-hmm. Makes sense. What about it?"

"Well . . . it's about yours." I knew as soon as I said it, I should not have. My face, my ears, my whole head turned red. Cook lifted the hand that he'd been resting on my shoulder so he could steer my head left and right. I bent my head low as I knew he was going to clout me a good one. I reckon I deserved it, too.

Cook never did hit me, though. He chuckled. "Relax yourself. I figured it was something like that. You might have noticed I am a black-skinned man. Well, my own dear mama told me that makes me special. The curly hair's part of being a black man, I guess. Now that's my mama's story. And a man ain't a man who goes against his own mama. You understand?"

I shrugged, and decided I should have nodded, but it was too late.

"What's that mean?" He stopped cutting. I didn't say anything. "You know your mama, boy?"

I didn't say anything for a moment or two. Then I said, "She died pushing me out, is how my Granna said it happened."

Cook made a sound, and covered it with a cough, but I heard it. When he spoke his voice was rough. "Your Granna, she raise you?"

"Yes, sir."

"Well, she did something right, because you use the word 'sir' a lot. You don't have to quite so much with me, though. Always with the boss, though, you hear?"

"Yes, sir. I mean, yes . . . well, what name should I call you?"

"Cook, everybody calls me Cook."

"Is that your name?"

He laughed, a big belly laugh. "Lord no, my own mama called me Clarence. But I don't mind Cook. Reminds me I'm good enough at something, other folks respect that. I don't know what more a man can ask for."

"Yes, sir. Cook."

"Cook is fine, Dilly." He sighed. "There, that's about all I can do with that knob you call a head. Now go take a look-see in the front window, and mind what I said about shaving. And Dilly?"

"Yes, Cook?"

"Don't be in too much of a hurry to grow into a man. Some things about it ain't too bad, but none of it's as good as you have it now, okay?"

I nodded.

"That batch of molasses cookies by the stove should be cooled off enough to eat. Go on and fetch one for yourself."

I was already up and making for the kitchen.

"One!" he shouted.

"Yes, sir. Cook!" I jumped through the back doorway, the door slamming behind me. I winced and froze in place. I knew Cook winced, too. But this time he didn't yell my name. Must be I'm growing on him.

I don't know what he meant about growing up. All I know is his childhood must have been a whole lot better than mine. I could not wait to be a full-bore ranch hand like Franklin.

CHAPTER SEVEN

I helped Franklin with Monty the horse twice more, and on that second time he asked me if I knew how to ride. He knew the answer, considering how I fell off his horse my first morning at the ranch. But it was kind of him to ask.

I'd been wanting to hear someone offer to teach me how to fork a saddle, which is what proper cowboys call it. I turned red and shook my head and looked at my feet.

"Why, Dilly, there's nothing shameful in not knowing something. Only in not learning how to do it."

"Oh, I want to learn how to ride," I said, nodding.

"Well, that's good. I can't think of a better horse for you to learn on, nor a better time than now."

"Now?" I stepped backward.

"Yep," he said. "Now. See that saddle, bridle, and such on the rack?"

I did, and nodded.

"Well, step on over here. Nobody's biting today. Monty has had his apple slice." Franklin winked and that was the first lesson I got in riding, which wasn't much on the riding but big on the saddling. I was familiar with tack, but never had the chance to do much more than rig up oxen and mules and horses in the traces.

I wouldn't have told Franklin this for all the money in a bank, but it seems to me the Indians have the right idea about such things. They will frequently climb up on a horse with little more than an old blanket beneath them and a rope bridle for steering the beast.

Now I'm not complaining. A fellow such as myself with not much experience riding horses is lucky to have a genuine cowboy like Franklin show him how to fork a saddle.

Climbing up onto Monty's back was a lot more work than I expected. I am of fair height for my age, near as tall as most grown men I have encountered, but it didn't seem to matter much.

"Unless you learn how to haul yourself up into the saddle, the longest legs in the world won't help you." Franklin said this as he shoved me up by the backside. He's a powerful fellow and nearly sent me over the saddle and off the other side of Monty, who didn't look concerned by all the tugging and pulling and dragging going on along his back and belly.

Franklin thought the same thing, because he said, "Lucky for us ol' Monty is one forgiving beast. He's been saddled more times than either of us can count."

He helped jam my boots into the stirrups and adjusted them so my knees weren't up around my earlobes. He said, "Okay? Let's go."

He led the horse around and around the corral, him standing near the center by this post with a worn groove around it near the top. He said it's called a "snubbing post," where they wrap lead lines when they train young, unbroke horses.

All this horse business was a complicated thing, but I reckoned it was worth learning more than anything else. At least it was to me. I had wanted to ride a horse longer than I'd been at the Hatterson Ranch. Ol' Monty wasn't mine, but that didn't much matter to folks there.

We repeated that afternoon's ride once more, a few days later, and it was almost as good as the first. About an hour in, Franklin tossed the rope up to me. I was riding on my own, no help nor guidance from him, except for what he told me.

I rode around and around the corral, not too close to the rails. Once in a while I wondered, if I tumbled off the horse and landed on a rail, how I might break my back, and then where would I be? Dead as dead can make you.

But as I gained in my confidence, that thinking didn't bother me. It must have showed on my face, because Franklin smiled— not an easy thing to see behind them big moustaches of his. "Well, Mr. Dilly, seems to me you are now on your way to being a full-bore cowboy. A few more lessons and you'll have her licked."

"You really think so, Franklin?" I was nearly out of breath, though I can't figure why, as Monty was doing all the work. I was setting on his back, bouncing up and down.

"Easy on the bouncing, Dilly. Ol' Monty can only take so much hard riding these days."

"Am I hurting him?"

"Nah, but relax yourself a little. If he bucks you off, I expect I'll one day be President of the United States."

Took me a few seconds to understand what he was saying. I relaxed and he was right, the ride smoothed out. Along about that time, Monty slowed down until he was barely walking. I nudged him in the ribs with my bootheels and made those kissy-clicky sounds I heard Franklin and the other men make when they wanted their horses to get along. But it didn't work on Montgomery.

"What's wrong with him?" I said.

Franklin laughed. "Nothing a good nap won't cure. He's done in for today, Dilly."

"Oh. Well, I guess I'll go cut wood."

I tried to guide Monty over to the gate, but he stood still with his head down as if he was listening to the dirt.

"That horse can be a stubborn old thing. Tell you what, Dilly.

Slide down off him and lead him over. Once he sees you mak-ing for the gate, he'll perk up."

So I did. And he did. "Now why do you suppose he's got fire all sudden-like?" I said, even though I knew the answer.

"Monty wants his stall. But after you lead him back in and strip off the saddle, give him a good rubdown." Franklin leaned close. "And dose him with a handful of oats, okay? But don't let the other horses see, nor the other men, for that matter. Or they'll all wonder why Monty gets special treatment. Can I leave you to do all that, Dilly? I have a couple of chores that need doing this very afternoon and I can't put them off any longer."

I nodded and stroked Monty's neck. "You bet."

Franklin clapped my shoulder a couple of times. "You're a top hand, Dilly. I appreciate it. See you at supper."

I led him into the barn and spent an extra couple of minutes rubbing Monty down. He seemed to like it and stretched and shivered now and again. Made me wonder if having a saddle on your back is painful. I can't think it is a pleasant experience.

And you plop a full-grown person on top of the saddle and have that person thrash around and whomp on your belly and whip on you to go even faster. And have something jammed in your mouth, and that same big person yarning away telling you to go left or right or in circles or up hills and down slopes . . . Why, I started to feel bad about it all.

"Sorry, old fellow," I said, and patted him a last time before I led him into his stall. I gave him those oats, which he enjoyed about as much as I enjoy a plate of food. Which is a lot.

I watched him eat for a minute, then I really had to go. "You're a top hand, Monty. For a horse."

Monty snorted and flicked an ear. I reckon in horse talk that means thanks.

Chapter Eight

I'd been at the Hatterson Ranch for three, four weeks when I first saw the night riders. Well, that's what I called them. It sounded more exciting and dangerous than calling them a bunch of ranch hands with their bandanas pulled up over their faces. I didn't recognize any of them, but Cook said they were from other ranches. He told me to shush myself.

He didn't look at me, which let me know something. He never tamped me down without giving me his look, the one where those two big woolly-worm eyebrows of his meet in the middle and droop down like they are set to square off in a pugilistic match. (I learned that word from Franklin. It means "boxing," or the "manly art," which still didn't mean a thing to me. Seems to me men could come up with something a little more noble and artistic to do than fight.)

So I nodded and stood beside him, watching the same thing he was watching. At dusk, those hands from nearby ranches came barreling in on their horses. They wore dusters and their hats tugged low, though it wasn't sunny.

It was after supper and none of the hands were out on the porch. I knew we weren't to have our usual nightly chin-wag, as Franklin called it, although he didn't usually do much talking himself. On other nights Pedro broke out his harmonica. It's a pretty sound, slow and soft, like the sounds I hear when I watch a sunset by myself or see a far-off duck on a pond.

I hadn't seen one of those in a while, though. Not too many

ponds out near the ranch. I told myself I would ask Cook if he knew where the closest pond was at.

I expected he would call that one of my "annoying" questions. He said that a lot. Sometimes I asked questions to hear him sigh and tell me to stop being annoying. He'd mumble about how that'd be like telling a beaver to stop chewing wood.

I didn't dare ask questions as the guests arrived. The way he'd told me who they were also told me he wasn't in a mood to talk.

Franklin and one of the other men, Clement, I think his name was, walked toward us leading their saddled mounts. They stopped before the cookshack and Cook went down to meet them. At the bottom of the steps he turned and pointed at me. "You stay put, Dilly. This is man's business."

I pouted by myself on the porch. The men were talking together, low and even. I hooked an arm around one of the posts and leaned out over the steps as far as I could. My feet were staying put, I'd not taken a step. Didn't matter, Cook looked over at me and said, "I wasn't fooling, Dilly."

"Yes, sir," I said, and inched back into the dark part of the porch and sat where Franklin usually sits. It was mighty hard not to jump down there and ask what they were talking about. I knew at least in their eyes I wasn't a man yet. But I worked the same hours they all did, and I'd been there for a long spell, I figured I had a right to know what was happening.

I'd almost made up my mind to walk up to Cook and Franklin and Clement and the other hands gathering in the group. Then I got a better idea.

I walked inside. The door was propped open so I didn't have to fight with that. When it's closed that thing squawks something awful. By then it was nearly dark, still light enough that I could see where the nearest bench was, which told me where the table was. I inched around the end, careful not to knock into the chair, and made straight for the back door.

This time I did not let it slam. It's a squawker, too, but only if you open it full wide like Cook has to, on account of him being such a big man. Me, I'm not carrying what he calls his "winter weight," even though it was summer when he told me that. I gentled it open and slipped outside, easing the door shut behind me.

I hugged tight to the backside of the cookshack in the direction of the big house. I knew if I angled along the end of the building and stuck to the shadows, I would hear what they were talking about. That was my plan. And it worked out that way, too, for a time.

What I heard was Franklin's voice, which you can tell apart from the other men because he talks slower than them. I came to learn that's because he was careful about what he was saying. Plus, his voice was deep. I guess that's because he was tall. But Cook's voice was deep and he wasn't as tall as Franklin.

It also let me know they'd moved and I was a whole lot closer to them than I thought. I peeked around the end corner of the building and saw eight men there. Some of the faces weren't familiar to me. I pulled my head back into shadow, like a scared turtle. Cook was closest to me, close enough for me to reach him in a couple of strides and tap him on the back. Maybe I could spook him. But it was not the time.

Plus, he'd whup me good, I knew it. He hadn't yet, but I had a picture in my mind of that big wooden spoon swinging toward my head, arms, backside, thighs. The meaty part, that's where adults like to hit because it stings like the devil.

Franklin said, ". . . they'll likely want to deal with the sheepmen in harsh terms—"

Earl interrupted him. I knew it was him because when he was worked up, which was most of the time, his voice got high and squawky, like the front door of the cookshack. "You bet we'll deal with them in harsh terms! Those foreigners ain't got no right to be here, their grass rats are ruining the range!"

"I think we ought to let the bosses decide what it is they want to do about the sheepmen. I was talking with Boss yesterday and he said he'd be open to an amicable solution. Now I think that—"

"Amicable?" said Earl, his voice going all squawky again. "You mean peaceful? That time is past, Franklin. Only thing those fools understand is hard words and harder treatment." That got a good half-dozen voices saying, "Yes, yes" and "Hear, hear." Sounded as if more of those folks were thinking like Earl than they were like Franklin.

Over the last few weeks I'd heard more and more such chatter among the men out on the porch at night. The night before, they were saying things that weren't favorable about the sheep ranchers hereabouts. How they were ruining the land for the cattle.

Cook told them he'd heard cattle won't eat where sheep have grazed, and Franklin said that sheep eat the grass so low it burns off. I imagine that's why Boss spent so much money on barbed-wire fencing and had men spending their days stringing it up everywhere I could see. It looked like rough work, as their clothes were all snagged with little holes and at night they were forever mending them by lamplight while they smoked and talked. Some of the men complained how it wasn't the sort of ranching they'd signed on for.

That got others of them worked up and they had a set-to there on the porch. The only thing that calmed it was when Cook brought out a big ol' crock with a cork on top and a loop handle. I knew what that was. Farmer Torbenhast kept one in the barn. He didn't think anybody knew about it, but one night I popped out the cork and took a sniff. It smelled bad, near as bad as a billy goat in rut. But I knew it was liquor.

Cook uncorked it. "I am willing to share my beloved jug of squeezins if you all agree to stop this infernal bickering tonight, and for a few nights running. It's getting foolish, Hatterson hands turning on one another like hydrophoby dogs. I won't have it, at least not on my porch. Agreed?"

Those men must have been more thirsty than they were up for snarling and bickering, because they all shut up tighter than a rain-swelled knot. Cook nodded, swigged from the jug, and passed it around. It came to Franklin, he glugged, looked at me, winked, and passed it clear over me. "Give it a couple of years, Dilly."

"Yeah, kid," said Earl. "You sample this, you're liable to stunt your growth." They all seemed to find that funny. I pretended to laugh, too, but I felt my ears burning up. Good thing it was dark.

The jug made it back to Cook. He swigged again, hefted it up and down, pooched out his bottom lip as if he was considering something important, then passed it around once more.

That was the night we got two songs on Pedro's harmonica, and not the slow, sad songs, either. Then Earl, to his credit, sang a song he said would be bawdy. He had a pretty voice for a man. I listened for the bawdy parts and didn't hear a one.

But on that night when the hands from other ranches showed up, I knew something was different, something that Cook couldn't fix with his jug. There was more talk, some of it got loud and fast, as if whoever was talking had to keep on with it, and not let his voice get trod upon by the other fellows.

The door to the big house opened wide. I heard boots on gravel walking closer, and I risked a peek again.

Boss walked out of his house and stopped at the group of ranch hands. Behind him came two other men. One was younger and downright fat, the last was a tall man, nearly as tall as Franklin, but thin like a fence post. They joined Boss.

83

By then the group must have had two dozen men. They had tied their horses to the low, fancy fence that lined the roadway up to the big house.

"Now boys," said Boss. "Simmer down." He held up his hands before him. It took a few seconds, but the group quieted. I noticed Boss was heeled, which I learned meant he was wearing a gun. Franklin said to make like a dry rag and soak up all the learning I can in life, so I gave it my all.

One day I told him I wanted to be a cowboy. He didn't laugh at me like other folks might. Instead, he nodded. "Okay. If that's the path you want to follow. But make certain you know you can always choose another path." That was nice of him to say, but why would I do that?

Boss continued. "I'd say by now you all know what we're here for. The sheepmen," he said the word as if it were a bitter thing he couldn't wait to get out of his mouth, "are closing in. They have moved into the valley. Our country, the country that me and Rod Delahanty here, and young Ben's father, Will Chase, settled back when Wyoming was nothing but a nubbin of a territory!"

It went on like this for some time. I wasn't bored, but my eyes roved here and there, inspecting the crowd. I wished Cook would have moved to one side or the other, as he was blocking my view. But I wasn't keen on tapping him on the shoulder and asking him to shift himself. I'd be in plenty of trouble if I made a peep, or if my boots clunked the building, or a board near me creaked from being sprung and dry, which they all were.

I let my eyes do the moving and pretty soon they wandered to the big house, off to my left. The porch was lit from a single oil lamp on a table and beside it, leaning against a post, half shadowed, much like myself, stood Myra. Something about her was so pretty at that moment.

She was doing the same thing I was. I saw the light reflect off her eyes as she turned and stared at me. I swear it. I should have been afraid that she'd point at me and yell something like, "Stop! There is a traitor and a sneak in our midst!" And all those cowboys would turn and stare in my direction.

Cook, being closest, would reach out a big ol' hand, snatch my shirt, and rattle me. But her eyes kept roving past me, and I knew she was feeling about like I was, spying on the situation, trying to figure it out. Maybe a little nervous, too.

Boss kept on talking. "When we moved here, there wasn't much but open country and redskin savages out to peel our hair from our heads and our hides from our bones. We built up this land, hard won, I tell you. You all are here by choice, and we were, too. But we had a stake, something more we were fighting for than monthly pay. We built up our herds of cattle from nothing at all. A few rogue beasts and a hat full of hope. And now look at it."

Folks murmured as if he'd said something grand.

"Why, Timmy O'Linn." Boss nodded and pointed toward the crowd. "You been here a long ol' time, came in as a youngster with your family moving westward. They chose to keep on rolling and you chose to stay. I know Ben gave you a place on his ranch. And since that day you've had a roof over your head, grub in your belly, and good mounts. And I hear tell you and a certain pretty girl from town are stepping out."

Boss smiled and nodded as joshing sounds rose up from the men. I couldn't see Timmy O'Linn, but I imagine I'd be red-faced if Boss said such things about me. And then he did.

"Why, some weeks ago, we had our own foundling turn up on our doorstep, so to speak. Kid was rough around the edges, but he had a spark, a look about him that made me want to keep him on. He's a solid worker and one day he might make a top hand. Am I right, Dilly?" That's when Boss turned and faced me, or rather where I was standing, in the shadows.

85

I stiffened, froze up solid. Didn't even breathe.

"Answer the man, boy," said Cook.

I didn't dare.

Boss said, "He's shy."

The men laughed and Boss kept on talking. He went on about the sheepmen, how they were a blight, whatever that is, on the land and a blight on the people. How they were most of them something called Basques, and how they were set on destroying everything Boss and his old ranching friends had worked so hard to build up.

"And that, my friends, is the short tale about why we have been fencing off our range. Lord knows we didn't want to do it. We all got along. We know each other's brands. We all work together at roundup. Our cattle don't overgraze the land or spread disease. So, if you agree with me and Delahanty and Chase, mount up. If not, stay here and tend to your knitting. Then find a new occupation, because you sure ain't cut out to ride for any brand in these parts."

A cheer went up among the men and a few of them even tossed their hats in the air. It was an odd sight. But I tell you, it made me feel good. I felt like whooping it up, too. Wouldn't have hurt anything, as everybody knew who I was and where I was standing anyway. But I kept my mouth shut. Didn't mean I wasn't smiling. I felt my heart bump-bump-bumping in my chest. I guess you'd call that pride. Boss said those nice things to all those people about me. Me. Orville Dillard Junior.

The group loosened and the men went for their horses, talking with each other as they walked. The last man standing where they'd all been, besides Cook, was Franklin. He stood close by, and I could see his face in the lantern light. He wasn't smiling. Cook said something low to him and Franklin shook his head and walked to his horse. I think it was the big bay.

Cook turned around and looked at me, his hands on his hips.

I stood up straight, didn't know what else to do.

"Well, boy?"

"Uh . . ."

"Yeah, *uh*. What do you think? We didn't see you creeping around back here?"

"Yes, sir. I mean, no, sir."

He chuckled and plopped a hand on my shoulder, and steered me around the back of the building. "Let's us go have a snack, call it a night."

I was relieved. "Where are they all headed, Cook?"

The big man sighed. "Going to . . . discuss things with the sheep folks."

"What sort of things?"

"If you were listening to Boss, you can figure out the answer to your question."

I thought on that, and nodded. "Yeah, I guess so. Sounds like those sheep folks need to leave. They don't have any right to be here."

"Well, now that's not true, Dilly. This here's open range. According to the law anybody is welcome to graze their critters on this range."

"That's what Franklin said, too. But that doesn't make sense. Boss said . . ."

"I know what he said. Look, let's get us a bite and have us each a quiet think. I have a few things to sort through in my own head about all this. Okay?"

"Okay, Cook." A few seconds later, I couldn't help myself. "Cook?"

He sighed as he scratched a match and lit the kitchen lamp. "Yeah, boy."

"Franklin didn't look none too happy when they rode out."

"No, he did not. I expect he's thinking hard on this matter about like we are."

I nodded and drizzled molasses on a crust-end of bread and thought back on what Boss had said to the group, and on what he said about me.

Later, with Cook snoring away like a big ol' bull on his cot, I thought about Myra as I fell asleep. I hoped none of the other ranch hands saw her as I did tonight. So pretty with the warm honey-glow from the oil lamp lighting up her crossed arms, the side of her face, her pretty, brown braid draped over her left shoulder.

As sleep tugged at my legs, my arms, and finally my eyelids, I wondered what Myra thought of the sheepmen.

CHAPTER NINE

Breakfast the next morning was a quiet affair. Even the sounds of the men chewing flapjacks, cutting ham, belching, breaking wind, and slurping coffee were all less boisterous than usual. The men ate, but only one or so helpings apiece, not their usual two or three. I didn't dare ask why because Cook gave me a narrow-eye stare and said nothing. I kept my mouth closed tight.

Oddest of all was when Franklin, who would normally show up on time to meals, came in about halfway through. The room was near-silent before he came in, and after, it was stone still. He walked over to his place at the table, stuck between Earl and a moody fellow, name of Manny.

Earl wasn't partway through his stack of flapjacks, but he stood up, tugged his napkin from under his chin, and dropped it on his plate. Then he left the cookshack.

It was an odd moment, but it got odder, because as Franklin set down at his place at the table, all the other men pushed away from the table and they left, too.

A couple of them, Clement and Horace, looked around at the others, and were turning red like I tend to in situations when I'm doing something I might regret. But they couldn't have regretted it too much, because they left. Pretty soon it was me and Franklin and Cook, all looking at each other like we each should know something more than we did.

Cook poured Franklin's coffee. "What are you going to do now?"

The tall cowboy sipped and set down his cup. "To be honest, I wasn't sure before I walked in here. But I am now."

Cook regarded him a moment, then nodded. "Yeah, I figured. Okay, then. I'll pack you some trail food."

Franklin started to tell him not to, but Cook said, "Don't you think of telling me my own business, now."

Franklin smiled for the first time since he'd come in. "I'd like to talk with Dilly, Cook."

Cook shrugged from the stove, his eyes on something in the big stewpot. Likely it was more beans. It's always beans. I know Cook says beans stick to your innards, and help get you through a day's work. But me, I would prefer to have myself a day when all I had to eat was fluffy cake with some of Cook's chocolate confection on top.

"Dilly, why don't you lend me a hand in the barn for a few minutes." Franklin stuck a bite of ham in his mouth but didn't appear to enjoy the chewing part. He held the door for me and we walked to the barn.

We passed the bunkhouse, where most of the hands were out on the porch loafing, which never happened at that time of day. A few of them looked our way, none too kindly. Earl made a show of spitting, and turned away. If Franklin noticed, he gave no sign.

As we made it to the shade of the barn, Franklin walked to his horse's stall and draped his arms over the door. "Dilly, do you recall what I said about riding for the brand?"

"Yes, sir."

He looked at me. "Well, I've ridden as far as I can for this brand. Now I need to go."

I wasn't sure why, but I had a guess. I hoped I was wrong. "Why?"

Franklin sighed. "It's this blamed sheep war."

"What's that got to do with you, Franklin?" I picked at the dusty top of the feed bin with my fingertip. My nail was dirty. If Cook saw that he'd make me wash again.

"It's only going to get worse. Boss and men like him figure they worked too hard building up what they got to go sharing with other folks, no matter the right or wrong of it."

"But the sheep are eating down the grass, ruining the land." I looked at him. Perhaps I could convince him yet. "Boss says they spread disease, too."

Franklin smiled and tipped his hat back. "See, they got to you, too."

"What do you mean?"

"They won you over, made you a believer in their side of things." He leaned toward me, folded his hands on the door before him, and looked at me. I don't believe I ever saw him so serious. "Look, Dilly. The only thing you have to know about this is that there's right in this thing and there's wrong, good and bad. You don't want to be on the bad side of it when it goes deeper south than it already has. Stay on the edges, Dilly, and light out if it gets worse. Above all, trust Cook. He won't steer you wrong. He's a good man."

Franklin laid a saddle blanket on the horse. "It's going to get bad before it gets better, Dilly. But it will get better."

I jammed my cuff in my eye, not caring that I was crying before another man. "What about riding for the brand? You said . . . you said . . ." And I shook, feeling angry and raw and sad and left alone again, all at once.

Franklin hefted his saddle up onto the bay and leaned his arms across it. "It's true, if you're drawing pay from a man, you're obliged to do his bidding. That's why I have to leave. But bigger than that, Dilly, a man has to be true to himself." He tapped my chest with one of those long fingers. "In here." He tapped my forehead. "And here."

I didn't know what to say. I wiped my leaking eyes and tried to figure out why I wanted to hit Franklin, maybe the only friend I ever had.

He turned back to his saddle. "Unless there's something wrong with a man from the start, deep inside he knows right and he knows wrong. The only thing he has to do when the time comes is make the right choice."

"How do you know?"

"You just do." He jerked down on the cinch and looked at me. "You know already, Dilly. You're smart, smarter than you allow yourself to believe. You don't need me to explain it."

None of this made sense to me. How could everybody else at the Hatterson Ranch be on the wrong side? The sheepmen were killing off the land, they were taking what they had no right to take. Everybody said so. More woollies than people, than cattle, than anything. And when they moved on, there wasn't much left but stubble that baked off, left nothing for the cattle to graze.

"If it's going to get better, why aren't you staying?" My voice rose and cracked. "You said a man has to ride for the brand."

Franklin sighed and rubbed his hand across his moustaches.

"Didn't you?" My voice sounded smaller to me, more desperate.

He nodded. "I did, yes. But we're talking in circles here, Dilly. I also told you about being your own man, about doing what you know to be the right thing, didn't I?"

"I don't want you to go, Franklin!" I blubbered and snotted on myself.

"Oh, Dilly." He put a big hand on my shoulder, but I shook it off. I should have left, but I stood there like a big, red-faced, knob-headed fence post and looked at my stupid boots.

"Take me with you." I looked up at him. "I won't be any

trouble. I can ride and I . . . I wouldn't bother you at all. I fended for myself for a long time, I know how to fish and . . . and . . ." I wanted to say more, so much more. I believe I could have spouted reasons for a whole hour why he should take me with him. But I saw his answer on his face and I knew it wasn't any good.

He let out a long breath and shook his head. "I can't, Dilly. I'm not sure where I'm headed, and I have enough trouble keeping myself out of harm's way." He smiled, hoping I would, too. But I didn't. Couldn't.

"Dilly," he said from his full height, looking down at me, with kind eyes and a flared look to those big moustaches. "I am not your father, you understand?"

The barn was quiet and I looked up at him, thinking he was waiting for me to say something. But he stood there with his head leaned back as if he was inspecting the rafter beams. But his eyes were closed. He spoke again, softer this time. "I have things I need to do, Dilly. Places to see in this world. I stayed here longer than I intended anyway. Promise me you won't stay longer than you should, you hear?"

He made to touch my shoulder again, but stopped, remembering how I shook off his hand before. I wished he had patted my shoulder one more time. I felt like a fool.

"You're a good man, Dilly. Don't become the bully."

He looked at me again. I looked back at him, felt my ears and face turn redder, redder than they've ever been in all my days. Then I said something to him that I have never said to another person before or since.

"I hate you."

I said it quiet, but my eyes showed him I meant it and my hands hung down as fists. But I didn't really mean it. Not inside, where it counts. I don't know why I said it, but if it was said to hurt the man, I surely did that.

I walked out of the barn without looking back. I should have, I know that. I owed that man more than I could count on ten hands. But I said it and so help me, the stubborn patch in my nature wouldn't let me turn.

I should have kept on walking up that mountainside behind the ranch, save myself and everybody there a world of headache. Up and over and kept on going, see what was on the other side. I could have, too. Like that Christmas night back at the Torbenhast farm, when I walked on out of there and never looked back.

But I didn't go up that mountainside behind the ranch. I turned right and walked back to the cookshack. I stayed on at the Hatterson.

CHAPTER TEN

Boss stood outside in the hot dirt, his arms crossed on his chest. Myra was back behind him, twenty feet or so, hugging herself, looking down at the ground. Even then, when things were happening that I didn't want to happen, she looked pretty.

Boss stared hard-eyed at Franklin, gritting his teeth. "It's not too late, you know. You can make amends for what you did last night."

"Me make amends?" said Franklin in a louder voice than I'd ever heard him use. "For what I did? Seems to me you have the wrong end of the stick, Boss."

It was as if Franklin had punched the little burly man in the chest. Boss stepped back once, caught himself, and bulled forward five paces before he stopped, finger pointed up at Franklin. There wasn't a stride between them. "I am no longer your boss. That's the way you want it, anyway. You've been paid and you deserve nothing else from me, you hear? You're a traitor. A sheep-loving traitor! Now get off my ranch, off my range!"

Franklin nudged the horse forward until he was standing beside Boss, who didn't back down an inch. His chest was working pretty hard and his face was dark, like blood.

Franklin leaned down, and other than a cow bellowing for its calf, way off in the pasture behind the stable, there was no sound except for that dry twisting of Franklin's saddle leather. "Take care of the boy."

"You mind your own business before I shoot you myself! I

95

took him in, didn't I? He's none of your affair now. Get gone!"

Franklin sat up and looked at me. He didn't say anything, but I saw that same old kindness in his eyes, the same Franklin I first met at the ranch gate so many weeks before.

He nodded at me and I felt like I should say something or do something, run over and tell him to stop being bull-headed. I wondered if that was what everybody was waiting for—maybe it was a test nobody told me about, something about becoming a cowboy. But I knew that was a thing a child will think. Wishful nonsense and nothing more.

That's when an odd thing happened. Earl, who I hadn't known was standing beside me, laid an arm around my shoulders, like we were pards, which is what Franklin called friends. I looked back up at Franklin and I saw something in his eyes change. He kept looking at me, but I could tell he didn't like seeing Earl be chummy to me.

I felt my face go even redder, hotter, and my eyes clogged up with tears and I didn't care. I looked at my big feet, even when I heard Franklin's horse turn, walk a ways, then trot up the lane.

I only looked up again when Earl shouted, "Traitor!" beside me. I shrugged out from under his arm and stood watching Franklin ride away.

If Franklin heard Earl, he didn't show it. His back stayed tall and straight, like how he showed me to ride. His tall hat made him look even taller and straighter. I thought then and I still think the same, all these years later, that what a cowboy ought to look like is what I saw riding away from the Hatterson Ranch that day.

CHAPTER ELEVEN

I was holed up on my bunk in the dark back corner off the kitchen. I tried to keep silent, but Cook heard me. He sat down on the edge of the bunk and rested a hand on my shoulder. "It's all going to work out, Dilly. You calm down."

"What did he do, Cook? What did Boss mean?"

Cook sighed. "Boss, he's worked up about the sheepmen. Way he looks at it, this land is his because he was here first, though don't tell the Indians that. But he was here long before the sheep folks come through, free grazing their stock. Way he sees it is the same way them other bosses see it, Delahanty and Chase, they built up their ranches and they don't want anybody else to have at this land. Between you and me, that ain't legal. You see, it's all free land, open to all."

"I know, Franklin told me."

"Oh, he did, did he? Well, good, save me some wind. Last night was supposed to be a meet-up 'twixt the ranchers and the sheepmen, figure out a way to live peaceable together. But you saw the way those hands were riled up. Boss and the other ranchers, they never wanted no agreement that doesn't end up with the sheepmen and their woollies all leaving the county."

I thought back to the night before, how Franklin was the last one of them left in the group, looking anything but happy like the other cowboys.

"Franklin knew, didn't he?"

Cook nodded. "Yep, he suspected what all was going to take

place, but he decided he'd ride along to see if he could prevent something bad from happening."

"He was riding for the brand."

Cook looked surprised. "Yes, yes, in his own way he was, Dilly."

"Did something bad happen last night?"

"Started to. Way I heard it from Clement, some of the boys, I won't say who, rigged up a rope as a noose. They was set to hang a sheepman as an example to the others. Send a hard sign that things weren't going to get any better for the sheep ranchers, so they should up and leave."

"How come you didn't tell them to stop it?"

Cook winced almost like I'd smacked him, something I would never even imagine doing. "I wasn't there, Dilly. Besides, it ain't the right time. Each man has to decide for himself when that is. Ain't yet for me."

"When will be the right time?"

"Not sure, but if it should come, I'll know."

"But Franklin knew, didn't he?"

Cook nodded.

"And he stopped them last night?"

Cook nodded again. "That Franklin, he's a good man."

"Why couldn't I go with him?"

"Franklin has other things he needs to do. He's not your average cowpuncher. Heck, he stayed here longer than he wanted to anyway."

"He said that."

"You know why, don't you?"

I shook my head. I was less angry with Franklin, though I still felt like he gave up on me.

"He stayed on because of you, Dilly. That day you turned up? He'd been planning to light out the very next morning, but you showed up and he felt like he needed to make certain you were going to have a good footing under you before he up and left. Then the sheep mess got out of hand."

"If he liked me that much, why didn't he take me with him?"

Cook sighed again. He did that a lot around me.

"Look, son, life is a whole lot more complicated than you think it is. Not that you have to know that now, 'cause you don't. But don't think that because Earl patted you on the head, he's your friend now. Ain't but one person in the world Earl likes and that's himself. You'd do well to stay out of his trail, you hear?"

I didn't say anything. He made sense, but I'd had about enough of people making sense and telling me things that were supposed to be for my own good. I didn't want to hear any more of it.

"You hear me, Dilly?"

I looked at him and for the first time since I got there, I didn't answer him. I shook my head and walked out the back door of the cookshack. And I let it slam behind me.

CHAPTER TWELVE

The next day I moved out of the cookshack. Not that I had much to move—except for a spare shirt, I didn't own anything. Even the spare shirt was somebody else's. Another dead cowhand, I expect.

When Cook gave it to me some weeks before, he mumbled something about a stomping. I decided I did not want to know any more. The shirt was decent (even if it had been in a stomping), a pretty blue plaid with brown wood buttons. It had been mended on both sleeves and the cuffs. The collar was worn from rough whiskers. I do not have that trouble yet.

There was an empty bed in the bunkhouse, and I was of a mind to be a cowboy. Also, the other hands didn't much seem to care if I was there or not. I acted more angry than I was. Mostly because I was tired of people telling me what to do all the time. Mostly that was Cook.

I missed him, though, and felt bad about how I acted. I didn't know how to make things back into the way they were. I wanted to sit with him before bed and have him put out the molasses and biscuits and say things like, "I sure don't understand how you can keep stuffing food in yourself like that." He'd shake his head and blow across the top of his coffee, even though I know it wasn't all that warm, as he liked to let the fire pinch low when it's hot outside, which it had been of late.

I kept cutting wood for the kitchen. Mad as I thought I was, I didn't want him to have to go back to doing that. I knew how much work he had in a day's time.

Besides, everybody else was busy all day long with their tasks, and though I took on some ranch hand jobs about the place, like cleaning the horse stalls and making sure the fence around the bottom of the chicken coop was buried down in the ground so the varmints wouldn't get in, they weren't enough to fill my day.

But wood cutting and chopping, that's a full-time job. Especially for Cook's stove. He really likes to lay on the heat when he's cooking. I don't know how he stands it. He's always dressed in longhandles, woolen trousers, and a button-down shirt, with an apron tied on top of it all. And a hat on top of his curly black-and-silver hair. It's no wonder he sweats. Could be that's why he's so grumbly.

One afternoon I was out there sawing and chopping, like every other afternoon since I got to the Hatterson Ranch, and I did what I usually do when I get into the swaying movement of the task—I dawdled in my mind as I am prone to do, thinking on things that I knew could never be. I gave thought to owning my own ranch one day. Not a farm like the Torbenhast place, but a genuine ranch, where I would be a cowboy.

I pictured myself taller and wearing what Manny calls his "woolly" chaps—which Earl says is the best use for a sheep anybody's ever found—and I'd have a hat, finally, a tall one like Franklin's with a wide brim that curls in the front. And every morning, Monty the horse would be there, waiting for me. I'd bring him an apple, a genuine shiny-skin, red apple every day. I'd saddle him and we'd go on long rides and count the number of cows I own.

This day I was in the middle of that happy story when I felt like somebody was watching me. I eased up and turned, and there was Cook, standing inside the cookshack, peeling on a potato, catching the one long peel around the crook of his pinky finger one hand, the potato in the other.

Cook is very practical about his potato and apple peeling. I think it's mostly a game to him, but he does like to keep the peel in one long piece instead of what I do, which he called "attacking the heck out of the thing until it surrenders." My method, he told me, while eventually successful, wasted food and effort.

We stared at each other a few seconds. He looked like he was going to say something, and I know I wanted to say something. I'd been thinking of how to say I was sorry for the way I had been toward him, but I did not know how to do that. Not yet, anyway. Cook walked back inside, and I heard the same old floorboards squeak under his boots.

I pulled my shirt off the axe handle where it was hanging and wiped my face. I didn't feel like sawing on any more logs, but I also didn't have any other tasks that needed doing. Problem was, all of a sudden I didn't much feel like doing anything. Not even feeding Monty an apple slice or two. And now that I wasn't in the cookshack, those were harder to come by.

I got a dipper full of water from the bucket hanging by the back door. I was careful to be quiet about it, but I knew it wouldn't matter, Cook hears everything. While I was drinking, I saw the big house and wondered about Myra. Odds are she was in there, cooking or cleaning or doing whatever it was she spent her days doing.

It came to me that I might go on up to the big house and knock on that door and ask to look at the library. After all, Cook and Franklin did, and Boss had said I was welcome to read a book from his collection if I wanted to. So that's what I did.

I made it to the top of the steps when I saw the front door was open, wide enough for me to poke my head and shoulders in. "Hello?" I said it twice, louder the second time, but nobody answered.

What harm would it do if I pushed open the door and walked straight to the Boss's office, chose a book, any book would do, and went back out again? After all, the door was wide open. Well, not wide, but open.

I found myself in the middle of the hallway, stairs in front of me, made of logs split and polished fancier than any I'd seen in a house before. I didn't recall them from my first visit in there, but now I took a longer peek. I wondered about the upstairs, and guessed Myra had her own room somewhere up there.

The idea of that made me feel like when you take a long, cold drink from a mountain stream and it makes your teeth ache and ices a trail down your gullet to your innards.

I was about to turn toward Boss's office when I heard a voice. It was Myra's, so I stopped again. I wish to God I hadn't.

I could swear she was giggling. It was coming from down the left side of the hallway, behind a set of big wood doors that looked like the ones on Boss's office.

There it was again, a shout followed by a giggle. It was definitely Myra. It was a pretty sound, like water over rocks in a stream. In no time at all I walked to the end of the hall and stood outside the doors. I hard a low, mumbling voice, and the girl shrieked and said, clear as a July morning, "No, now stop it. I mean it now. Stop it!" But she giggled again.

I heard the low voice and she said pretty much the same thing one more time, but louder. I knew what I had to do, and I did it before thinking, which has gotten me into all manner of trouble in the past, and that didn't change here.

I had a sharp picture in my mind of bandits with their faces covered up with kerchiefs, robbing the place. Maybe Myra was giggling because she was nervous. I have done that myself. All I knew was that she was in trouble and I had to help. I grabbed the door handle and thumbed the latch.

The first thing I saw when I shoved open the door was a man not much taller than me with his back to me. Behind him, but not covered up by him, stood Myra. She was backed up to a long worktable in the middle of what was obviously the kitchen. I saw a big, black cookstove, all fancy with nickel trim, and a long countertop with a sink against the wall to my left.

Myra stared at me and I saw that her shirt was hanging loose from her skirts and the man's hand was up under there. I don't think he knew I was there because he kept making low mumbly sounds and was pushing forward while she leaned back away from him. Looked to me like he was trying to kiss on her. She'd stopped telling him no, stopped giggling, because she saw me and I saw her, our eyes staring at each other.

I am afraid I did another one of those dumb things I do sometimes. I said, "Oh, ah . . ." and I said it loud enough that the man heard. He whipped around fast and that's when I saw it was Earl.

I don't know why I didn't guess it was him before that. Could be because he was without his hat. Mostly I didn't expect to see him in the big house.

"Dilly, what are you doing? What do you want, boy?"

He came at me, and he was fast. It wasn't any time at all before his fist popped me a good one. I think he was aiming for my face, but he hit my shoulder, then my neck. Might be because he's not any taller than I am. In fact, I think he might be shorter, because his boots have sizable heels on them.

His punch hurt, but I reckon mine hurt more. I didn't even think but hit him back, quicker than I thought I could, too. And I got my second surprise of the day. He spun around like he was dancing and fell over. He sat up again, shaking his head. The girl knelt by him, but he shoved her away.

I bent low and said, "Earl, I'm so sorry. I didn't mean it. I wasn't thinking. I'm sorry, Earl. I didn't mean to hit you, being friends and all."

He jumped up, rubbing the side of his head where I laid into him, and looked me up and down. He stuck a finger up almost into my nose. His face was real close and he was breathing hard, like he'd run around the corral a few times chasing a cantankerous mount (which sometimes happens to some of the cowboys).

His finger was shaking as much as his voice when he said, "I am through with you, Dilly, you big, foolish child. And make sure you understand between your big stupid ears, no orphan whelp was ever a friend of mine, nor of anybody else's hereabouts, you hear me?"

"But Earl . . ."

"I will lay you low, Dilly. You won't know when or where. You won't see it coming. You look out." He stomped past me and I heard the front door slam, his boots whacking hard on the steps.

Now that didn't really make sense because if I'm looking out, surely I will see something coming. But that notion didn't come to me right away. I was too bothered by what had happened to think much at all.

I stood there turning red. The girl moved and I rubbed at my eyes something fierce.

She stuffed her shirttails back into the top of her skirt, and walked over by me. "Please don't tell anybody. It was all my fault. I goaded Earl on. He's still your friend, he didn't mean what he said."

I nodded and didn't say anything, but I knew she was wrong. Earl hated me. He didn't have to say anything. I saw it in his eyes. With angry eyes like that, I don't know if he ever liked anybody.

She kept talking while she finished making herself look tidy again. Then she did something I will never forget. She put her hands on my cheeks and said, "You're a sweet boy, Dilly." She patted my shoulder and I figured that was when I should leave. All that and I never got a book to read.

CHAPTER THIRTEEN

The worst part of it came a couple of days later, before it was time to eat. The hands were outside the kitchen, loafing and waiting. I'd been keeping away from Earl, which was not easy since we all slept in the same bunkhouse. But I was down along the front side and he was off in a back corner. Still, I felt him staring at me. Nobody said anything about it, so I guessed he'd been tight-lipped about me hitting him, and why. That was fine with me.

As I said, we were all outside the cookshack, waiting for supper, when something shoved me hard from behind. I stumbled forward, landed on one knee, and looked around. It was Earl.

He was standing over me, looking about like he did that day in the kitchen. His eyes still looked like he wanted to kill me. His cheek was still red from where I'd hit him. Before I could say anything, he came at me, shouting that I'd been prodding him too much, begging for a fight.

He shouted, "I am here to oblige you, boy!"

I looked up quick at the rest of the hands on the porch, but they looked as confused as me. All of this happened fast, then things happened even faster. Earl stepped in close while I was still on my knee and punched my head once, twice, three times, from left to right and back again.

After the first pop I didn't hear so good. I think he hit my ear. I wobbled, down onto my other knee, and tried to push him away with my arms. It got hard to see, purple and fuzzy, and Earl was shouting the whole time about how I kept trying to get him to fight and how he didn't want it, and none of it was true.

I did what I always did when someone was whomping on me, usually it had been Mr. Torbenhast. I bent low, covered my head with my hands, and curled in on myself.

He grabbed me by the shirtfront and the buttons started to pop off. He kept on with it and spun me around with my shirt-tails in his hand and yanked hard on my shirt. I thought I heard it ripping and sure enough, it was in two pieces, one hanging off each of my arms like I had great cloth wings. Worst part, though, was what happened next.

I was stumbling around in a circle, on account of my eyes were swelling shut and my face was all rubbery feeling, and I saw blood drooling out of my mouth. I remember hoping Myra wasn't out there like she sometimes is, talking with everybody before a meal.

Everybody got quiet and Earl wasn't whomping on me anymore. That's when I understood. You see, there's a reason why I never took my shirt off in front of anybody other than me and myself alone.

It's because Mr. Torbenhast and the Gileads before him used to lay into me pretty regular with a strap, though Torbenhast also had a proper whip. I think it was a buggy whip he cut down. Doesn't matter. It stung like the devil, mostly on my back, some on my sides and belly.

I figured I deserved it, at least that's how I felt early on. After a few years, I didn't much think about it. I took the lashes and figured they'd heal over faster if I forgot about them. That was difficult, though. Had to sleep on my belly most of the time. I tried a salve Mr. Torbenhast had a tub of for the cows, but he saw I'd used some and laid into me for that, too.

That's when I learned that some things in life are best to

keep quiet about. They go away faster that way. But that's why my back looks as it does, all puckery and welted. I've seen enough of it looking back there and feeling it with my hands.

I heard voices coming closer, heard Earl make strangling sounds, and heard Cook shout, "You a man? You a man now, Earl? Huh? Why don't you fight a man then, instead of a boy. Come on, let's have it!" I heard two quick slapping sounds and somebody flopped to the ground.

I could not see much of anything, but I felt Cook close by. He's a big man and he smells of spice and sweat and his pipe and coffee, all at once. He lifted me to my feet. "Hush now, Dilly. Hush, hush."

I felt something on me, felt like Cook had draped a blanket or some such over my shoulders, covering my back. I later found it to be his apron.

"Come on now, Dilly. You come with me."

His big arm was around my shoulders and he all but carried me, though I recollect my feet touching the ground as if I was walking.

"Let's us take a walk, Dilly. Get ourselves around back here, cool off by the washbasin. Nothing like a little walk and some cool water to clear a man's head." He kept talking like that, rough and quivery.

Once he'd wiped off my face, I found I could see out of my left eye a little. I touched my face lightly with my fingertips. "Is it bad?"

"Could be worse, Dilly. Earl ain't a big man, so he don't throw a big punch."

He walked inside the cookshack and came out with one of his own shirts, which was far too big for me, but he rolled up the sleeves and buttoned the front. "Now, let's us take a walk."

"What about supper?"

He looked at me. "Don't tell me you're hungry after all that?"

109

I shook my head. "No, the men."

"Oh, they aren't about to starve. They'll fend for themselves, though I reckon they'll leave a mess behind. Come on, nothing like a walk in the hills to clear a man's mind."

By the time we got back down from our walk, it was near dark and the cookshack was quiet. The kitchen was not what I would call clean, but not too bad, considering the boys had been at it, feeding themselves from what Cook had on the stove. Beans and biscuits, likely. Cook made some mumbling noises and I felt bad, but he told me to sit at the table. He brought over a plate of cold biscuits and jam, a glass of milk for me, and a cup of coffee for himself.

We ate biscuits for a couple of minutes, then he said, "Something we have in common."

"What's that, Cook?"

"Your back. It's about the same as mine."

We sat like that for some time, me not eating and Cook not sipping his coffee, which I am certain had grown cold. After a while he sipped it, a little at a time as if it was hot.

"Cook?"

"Yeah, Dilly."

"Why?"

He looked at me and he knew what I meant. He breathed deep. "Some folks are hard from the start, Dilly. Might not even be their faults, but if they don't work at it, they never will change. Some folks get that way through living, start out kind as babies, and get hard as they go on."

"Like Earl?"

Cook nodded. "I expect he's fighting somebody who's always behind him. A mean pappy or mama. Might be what I did wasn't the best thing. In the middle of a moment like that, you don't always do the thing that's right. But you do the thing that needs doing."

110

"Sounds like something Franklin told me."

"Good man." Cook sipped his coffee. "Hope he finds what he's looking for."

Something bubbled up inside me, thinking about Franklin, and I knew I was going to cry again. I held a hand over my eyes as if I was looking toward something far off in the sun, but I kept my head low.

"What is it, Dilly?"

I shook my head. Cook didn't say anything.

"I didn't mean it, Cook."

"What's that?"

"I told Franklin something bad, I . . . told him I hated him." I looked at him. "But I didn't mean it."

Cook put one of those big hands on my shoulder. "Course you didn't, Dilly. You ain't lived long enough to hate. Besides, you're a good person. Trust me, I know."

"You think he hates me for saying it?"

"Who? Franklin? Naw, he's too smart for that, Dilly. Besides, he was a boy once, too, you know."

111

CHAPTER FOURTEEN

That night I stayed back in my old bunk in the cookshack. I did my best to make like nothing had happened, and I guess everybody else did, too. Even Earl, who looked about as bad as I did, what with his eyes all buttoned up by Cook, didn't pay me much attention. But I did catch him looking over at me now and again, staring. Hard to tell what he was thinking. I know he was looking at me because that meant I was looking at him. Which made me wonder how often he was looking at me when I didn't catch him at it.

A few days later there was a big commotion amongst the men at the table. I could tell it bothered Cook because he kept slamming pots harder and harder until I thought they would crack in two. The men caught on, though it took them longer than I thought, considering the ruckus Cook was raising.

Clement said, "Sorry, Cook." The other men nodded and didn't look at the big man. Cook grunted, but he didn't slam his pots around after that.

I took over my old chores at mealtime like I had done before I left in my huff.

When Cook took me for that walk after the fight, he kept talking. I didn't say much, but nodded now and again and said, "Yes, Cook," when I thought I should, but I'd never heard him talk so much. It was nice. He kept his hand on my shoulder like we were old friends, which I guess we were.

He told me a lot of things, some of them I swore I'd never

tell anybody, which is why I won't mention them here. But one thing he said was a lot like something he told me a while ago, and if Cook repeats himself, I learned it's wise to listen. He said, "Don't be in a hurry to grow up. It ain't all strawberries and fresh cream. It ain't all bad, neither. Let it happen as it should. Don't rush it, else you'll end up with a problem to sort out."

I been thinking on that, and I think it's useful for about anything: Let it happen as it should. Seems to me Boss was forcing something he shouldn't have by being so worried about the sheep folks. I'd been thinking a lot about them and about what Franklin said, and more importantly, what he did.

He tried to make sure everybody was talking. He said there wasn't much that couldn't be talked out. He also said that words were cheaper, and a whole lot less painful, than bullets. He was a wise man, was Franklin.

As I said, I was thinking a whole lot about the problems Boss and the other ranchers and cowhands were having with the sheep people. If what Franklin and Cook said was true, and I know it was because they don't lie, there was something I could do.

I didn't know what or how or when, but I knew I had to try, mostly for Franklin. Even if he never knew I tried, at least I'd know.

And that bit of thinking is what got me in the biggest trouble I had ever been in. The biggest trouble of my whole life. I talked with Cook one afternoon, before all the trouble started.

"Cook?" I said, sorting through another pan of beans. He's particular about his beans, only likes to cook with pintos. I have to rummage through them looking for little stones because he doesn't want any of the boys to crack a tooth on his cooking. *I'd never hear the end of that,* he told me once, early on, *so that's why you sort the beans. And that's all I'm going to say about it.*

You can bet I sorted those beans. So I was doing that one afternoon when I asked Cook a question. I never know how he's going to take it, but he seemed less surly than usual, so I asked. "How do you think this argument with the sheep folks is going to work out?"

Without even thinking about it, which he will do often, Cook said, "It will not end well for the sheep folks, I can tell you that much."

"Why?"

"Because Boss and his friends are rich men, got a whole lot of money. But more important than money, they got power. Owning land means you have power, power over whatever's on that land, be it man or beast."

I chewed on that for a minute. When I do that, I am prone to stopping whatever I'm doing so I can think proper, which I did. Cook gets flustered when I do that.

"You going to stand there with your mouth open, catching yourself a ranch full of flies, or are you going to sort my beans? I have to get them in to soak or we won't be eating a thing come tomorrow."

"Sorry, Cook. I was thinking."

"Oh, well, that's okay then. I can tell the boys come tomorrow that Dilly, he was thinking, so all they'll get for vittles is a few biscuits and syrup. I'm sure they won't mind."

I didn't want to tell Cook that it wouldn't be such a bad idea to rest the whistleberries now and again. The cookshack is one smelly ol' place after a meal. And when we wake up, too. Cook, he can fart up a storm, a big ol' mountain of a thunderstorm. I wasn't the only one who thought so.

Clement said between Cook's farts and snores, he might as well be a big boar grizzly. He didn't say that when Cook was around, though, else he would have gotten clouted on his ear by that big grizzly.

After a couple of minutes, Cook looked at me and said, "Why you asking that, Dilly?"

"I was thinking about something Franklin said."

"Oh? What was that?" He was listening, but he was also rolling out the biscuits between his hands. He pinches them off his big ball of sourdough, and rolls them in his hands, and sticks them in the big cast pot. I don't see how he can do all those things at once.

"He said something like, you know you're a man because you stand up for the good things in life, even if it scares you to do it. He said that going along with something, especially if you don't think it's the right thing to be doing, well, that makes certain you aren't a man."

"Dilly." Cook set down the biscuit he'd rolled between his palms. And walked over to me. "You aren't thinking of doing something foolish now, are you?"

"What do you mean?" I said, trying to sound as if I didn't know what he was talking about.

"I mean, I hope you aren't planning on doing the same thing Franklin did."

"What?" Did Cook think I was going to leave the Hatterson?

"Let me tell you something, Dilly. I heard the talk, how they're planning on paying the sheep rancher over in Mad Woman Valley a social call." He jerked his head over his right shoulder. "And I'll tell you now, you best not be with them." He wagged a big finger in my face.

He made me so angry I wanted to bite the tip of his finger clean off. But the moment passed. I knew he was right.

He said something that changed my mind back to where it was seconds before. He stuck that finger in my sniffer again and said, "Dilly, you listen hard now. I forbid you to go with them on their next night ride to that sheep camp."

The words were bossy sounding, but the way he said it and

115

the way he looked at me when he said it, they were kind. It was confusing, but I know he meant well. I didn't say anything.

"I'll tell you the truth of it, Dilly." He went back to rolling his biscuits. "It will not end well. Sheep will die, sure, that's happened from the start. And men get hurt, too. But this time," he looked around as if someone else was in there with us, listening from the dark corners. He leaned close and stared hard at me. "Men are likely going to die. You ever seen a dead man, Dilly?"

I didn't answer. I was thinking of my pap, who I hadn't thought of in quite some time. He didn't wait for me to say anything, anyway. Cook went on talking.

"What do you honestly think you can do, Dilly?"

I took a deep breath. "I could make a difference. Get them to talk, like Franklin said. Boss is a smart man. He owns all those books."

Cook looked at me as if I'd said something silly or cute. I didn't feel like I was silly or cute. I was angry. Why wasn't he willing to try to stop the foolishness?

"Owning books don't make you smart, Dilly, any more than owning a hat makes you a top hand or a recipe makes you a good cook. You understand?"

I didn't say anything.

"I said, 'Do you understand?' "

Finally, I nodded.

"Good," said Cook. "Now we best get those beans in to soak."

I nodded, but inside I was thinking of how I could prove him wrong, and prove that Franklin was right. I didn't have long to wait.

CHAPTER FIFTEEN

It wasn't but a week or so after the fight, when things seemed like they were settling down to be normal again, at least for me, when I overheard Earl and Manny talking about the ride they were going on the next night. It hadn't seemed like anything they were trying to keep quiet. In fact, they talked about it later on the porch. Cook argued some, but stood up and went inside, shaking his head.

The next night came and I planned to sneak out with the boys. Even if they discovered me, I could get far enough that they wouldn't turn me back. Cook wouldn't be happy, but I made sure in my mind his frowning face was smaller than Franklin's smiling face.

I knew it would be easy for me to blend in with the group, as there were at least two dozen riders milling about, most of them from other ranches. I recognized some, from the night of their first ride, as they sat their horses. Some stood by their mounts, talking and laughing. Most of them had what looked to be weapons of some sort strapped to their saddles.

I got scared, not only because I was going against Cook, but I also didn't know how I could stop all those armed men. I'd done a pile of things in my life that scared me plenty, so whenever I got in a situation that made my hands wet and my mouth dry, I forced myself to think back on one of those times I was most scared. I called to mind leaving the Torbenhast farm that Christmas night two years before.

What if he had caught me? For all I knew, Mr. Torbenhast might have laid into me so hard he'd kill me. *Think on that,* I told myself. And so I found Monty in the barn, and I saddled him up with the same old mothy blanket and mended tack Franklin said I could use. Said they were for anybody who needed them.

If I had known what would happen that night, I would have taken my spare shirt. Well, in truth, if I had known ahead of time what was about to happen, I don't know as I would have gone along with the cowboys that night. But I like to think I would have. If only to make Franklin proud of me. Which is silly, as he was long gone.

Before I mounted up, I found an old duster hanging on a peg in the stable. That's when I heard the big group of men riding out. I didn't want to be too far behind them, close enough to mix in, hopefully among hands from other ranches, in case some of the Hatterson hands saw me and knew that Cook didn't want me riding along with them.

I was set to pull on that duster, but it was true to its name, a dusty thing, caked with years of it. Smelled like mouse mess, too, but I needed it. So I ran into an empty stall and shook it hard.

It was so old I was afraid to get too rugged with it, lest it tear apart in my hands. It raised a fair cloud of dust, and I coughed up a storm. I tried to stifle it by wadding my shirt collar in my mouth. I tugged on that long coat, pleased to feel it fit, and more pleased to see it had a tall collar that age had only made stiffer.

I still didn't have a hat, so I unbent the collar as tall as it could go and fastened the top four buttons. That's all it had anyway. I guess the rest got chewed to nothing by mice or pack rats. The buttons that were there were gnawed, too, but they worked. The raised collar didn't look at odds with how the rest of the men looked, and I trotted ol' Monty up behind the last of the big group.

For the first time, I felt like a real cowboy.

The end of the ranch lane was in sight when a horse walked up alongside me and Monty. I looked over at the same time the rider looked over at me. It was Earl. Dang, I thought he was up front.

"Dilly." He said it like my name was something foul he couldn't wait to get off his tongue.

"Hi, Earl," I said, and I looked forward. But he didn't leave me be. He rode beside me. I heard his saddle creaking as he leaned closer.

Finally I had to look at him. He was giving me a hard stare. "Don't you never say my name again, boy." He pointed a finger at me, poking the growly words as he spoke. "I am nothing to you, you understand? I am not your friend, and I sure ain't a replacement for that traitor, Franklin."

"He wasn't a traitor," I said, but quiet. I imagine my red ears were louder than my voice.

"What was that?"

I shrugged, another habit I learned from Cook.

"That's right. And when we get there, you do whatever it is you think you have to do, but do it away from me." He looked like a crazed dog, his eyes cold and grim.

Up to then, I had thought nobody could be all mean, no matter what the dime novels want us to believe. But nobody could be all to the good side, either. We each have good and bad in us. That's how we get through the hard times and the soft.

Earl thought he was doing the right thing for Boss. He should have known it was wrong, but he didn't. That says more about the man than I can.

I didn't know how far we were going, but everybody got quieter as we rode. The light started to pinch out, too, even though it gets dark late here in summer. Light enough to see where you're walking when you're beelining for the outhouse, anyway. That's handy when you want to avoid snakes or skunks.

I looked at the other men and they were tugging kerchiefs up onto their faces. One of them was Boss. He saw me and pulled his kerchief back down as he angled over toward me. "I did not think to see you here, Dilly. You're a boy."

That was a hard thing to hear and I felt myself redden up. He said, "Well, no matter. No harm's going to come to you."

"Okay, Boss," I said, though I didn't feel as confident as I sounded. I let a moment go by before I cleared my throat. "Boss?"

"Yeah, Dilly." He sighed a little, like I was bothering him. I wouldn't have, but I needed to know a few things.

"What should I do? I mean, I'm happy to help with most anything."

"I know that, son. And I appreciate it."

"I don't know who we'll be talking with. I'm not much of a talker in front of folks I don't know, but I'm willing to try."

"That's good, Dilly, but there won't be much talking. Now keep quiet. We're nearly to the first stop. Follow me, but not too close. Here." He pulled free one of the axe handles I'd wondered about, lashed behind his saddle. "You hold onto that end and swing it down and away, like this." He demonstrated. "And hit hard. Hard! You mind?"

I nodded and he handed it to me. "Boss?"

"Yeah?"

"What are we hitting?"

He made a sound like the sounds Cook made when I asked too many questions.

"Sheep, Dilly. As many as you can and as hard as you can. Hit them here," he tapped his own head, dragged a finger up from his eye to his ear. "On a sheep's head, you knock him hard enough there, and you'll do some damage. If you don't kill it, you'll sure as shootin' addle it so it won't be of use to those foul sheepmen after that."

He pulled up his kerchief, clicked his tongue, and rode on ahead, leaving me and Monty walking along, me staring at the axe handle in my hand. At the end where the head had been, the wood was dark, like it had been dipped in something. I pulled it closer to my face and saw curly white hairs stuck to it. I knew it had been used before to do exactly what Boss told me to do with it.

"I thought we were going to talk," I said out loud, but the men were leaving me behind. For the first time, I saw they all were carrying clubs and ropes and guns. And that told me what I didn't want to believe—there wouldn't be much talking. What Cook and Franklin had warned me about. There would be beatings of men and killing of sheep. And I was in the middle of it.

CHAPTER SIXTEEN

A few of the men lit rag-topped torches, the heads whooshing bright orange in the dark. If I wasn't so scared, I would have thought the entire affair was pretty. But sheep were going to suffer, likely die. Men would get hurt, too. I heard Cook's words over and over in my head.

I have never tried to hurt an animal I wasn't going to eat. Even that makes me feel as if I should somehow be hurting, too. Never seemed fair that I could take the one thing that mattered most to a fish or a chicken or a rabbit, its life, and not at least feel bad about it.

I never could help it, I'd get to thinking that if I was in that critter's position, with a big goober like me looking down at me, like as not I'd fight and squirm and do my level best to get away. Or I'd give in and hope that the thing I knew was about to happen might somehow turn out better than it would. It never does, but it's a thought that might give a critter comfort in its last moment.

I could tell when we reached the first sheep camp, because the men slowed their horses and rode in a tighter group. I was on the far edge of it, but I think I saw Boss in the middle, pointing and waving his torch in different directions. Some of the men would nod and ride off slow together.

I also knew we were close to the first camp because I smelled the sheep, then I heard them. I have been around enough sheep to know what they look like and what they sound like and how dumb they are. Of course, I've met people who weren't much smarter than sheep. It's possible folks think that of me, too.

The horses weren't happy about the torches and kept grumbling and prancing in place, with the cowboys tugging on the reins and jerking them this way and that. I kept Monty back from the rest, in case he decided to join in. Though from the way he acted, he was as likely to fall asleep. He does not have a jumpy personality. I'm not even sure cannon fire would rile Ol' Monty.

Someone whispered my name. "Dilly—come on!"

It was Earl, and he didn't sound too happy to have to say it.

We rode hard up a treed slope and broke through thick stands of aspen and ponderosa trees, some of the branches raking my legs and arms, and I hoped Monty didn't get scratched up too bad.

There before us was the great crowd of sheep, their fuzzy bodies grayish in the dark night. I saw spots of hopping, dancing flame and was reminded of fairy stories an Irishman had told around a campfire many months before, when I was traveling. I forgot for a moment these were torches carried by the men.

Earl shoved his horse into mine and we rode straight into the middle of the jumping, bleating, running sheep. He rode past me, swinging his club and shouting along with the rest of the men. At first I thought they were going to scatter the sheep and make a big show of it all.

Somehow, I still didn't think these men, many I knew, would kill sheep for such a paltry reason. But as I rode forward, I saw holes in the sea of sheep and realized they were knocked-down beasts, laid low by Earl and the rest of them.

I slowed Monty to a walk. Below my right boot was a downed sheep, but it wasn't dead or stunned. It was bloody-headed, and among the bleats and cries of the other sheep, I heard a bubbling scream coming from this sheep's mouth, its jaws working sideways to each other, bloody foam leaking out.

It was horrible. I saw more and more sheep down, twitching, their legs snapping at the air and kicking as if they were trying to run.

I looked at the club in my hand and I almost threw it, but I didn't want to hit an animal by accident. The sheep were everywhere, and I guided Monty through them. We walked into some by accident, but I don't think we hurt them. From the way he tensed up and jerked his head, I could tell Monty was as bothered by the situation as I was.

Some of riders with torches came back around toward us. The sheep turned and ran harder in a big group, circling around us once more. I nudged Monty, angling him off to the side to get away from the sheep. The trees we'd come from were over to my right.

The sheep ran faster and louder, jumping over each other, running in all directions at once, even under Monty. That's when he started kicking up a fuss. I'd never heard him worked up before, but I reckon that night he had cause to misbehave.

It was dark, too dark for him to see, I guess. I think he must have got tripped up over a downed sheep. I heard Monty neighing, and the torches off to my left fell away and I saw purple-black sky, and blinks of high-up light, stars, I think. I didn't feel him beneath me after that, and I hit the ground hard.

I'd fallen off my horse, and at the worst time, too. Sheep were everywhere, slamming into me. I felt the scrubby, bristly grass against my chin and my cheeks. I tried to get up to my knees, and heard a strange noise, odder than the bleats and shrieks of the sheep. Pretty soon I figured out it was me yelling words, all mashed together, like I was trying to shout over the sheep.

I shoved up to my knees and grabbed hold of the nearest

woolly. It was like grabbing a big, hairy head. I got one leg up under me and was working on the second when a new wave of sheep knocked me backward. Mostly they ran around me, but one ran on top of me like I was a floor.

I flipped over and figured if I laid there curled up with my hands over my head, I would likely be stomped to death, one little hoof at a time. That notion did not excite me, so I dragged myself along, shouting my gibberish words and trying to get a leg under me, all the while the sheep slammed into me, jumped over me, and walked on me. I thought I could see the trees, though they looked too far away.

I wondered why I could see them. The whole night was bright, and off to my left I saw the reason. Something large, as tall and big as a wagon, was on fire. I heard men shouting from all directions, and I saw the torches, fewer than when we rode up. That's also when I heard the first gunshots.

Who was shooting? I hoped none of the boys had been wounded, nor Boss, neither. But what if it was them doing the shooting? Clubbing sheep was bad enough, but bullets? I didn't have time to think more on it because another sheep stomped on my back, pushed me flat on my face one more time. Those hooves pounded like little fiery fists.

Sheep dung and dust and blood clouded me, and it all smelled hot and tasted awful. My mouth and nose were filled, and I think I bit the inside of my cheek when I landed.

I spit and crawled, blinking and shouting, not that it was doing any bit of good. Those dumb sheep kept on trampling me. They hurt like blazes and I knew if I lived through it, I'd see plenty of hoof-shaped dents and bruises all over me, head to toe. The big duster coat was more of a hindrance than a help, though I expect it did protect me some by being another layer of cloth between my body and the digging hooves.

My shoulder ached with each pull, but I forgot all about it

when I felt what I thought was a dead sheep lying in front of me. I decided I'd use it to curl up behind. I hoped it was big enough that the sheep would run around it and not over me anymore. I pawed it again and found it wasn't a sheep. It was a man.

Though the sky was lit by the burning wagon, I couldn't see who it was. He lay flopped on his side, and I fumbled my hands along him. I patted and felt boots, trousers, and a wide belt, coat, and a shirt.

"Hey!" I bent low and shouted it again as loud as I could. I guess the sheep were thinning out because I heard my voice. The man on the ground must have, too. He flopped onto his back.

The sheep were parting around us, and didn't look interested in trampling me or him anymore. He groaned, at least I think he did, and I felt his chest rise. I held a hand on the far side of his head in case the sheep decided to step on his face.

"Hey! You okay?" I shouted. It was a dumb question, but we were in a dumb situation. "Who are you?" I shouted, though it didn't matter which of the boys it was.

He said something, but I couldn't hear it. I bent my head over his face and shouted. "What?"

"Help me," he said.

Hearing those two words, somehow I knew it was not a cowboy. And that meant it was one of the sheepmen. I leaned close and looked at him. He had dark eyes. Heck, everything was dark. And he had a moustache, but he looked young and scared. His head was half covered in blood, and I knew he'd been clubbed like a sheep.

He stared at me and said something else. He needed help. I was trying to figure out what to do.

The crowd of sheep thinned and I saw the trees ahead, closer than I thought. "I'm going to drag you to the trees!" I shouted.

He closed his eyes and nodded. I muckled onto his arms, worked my hands up under his armpits, and tugged. That's when he shouted, a high, pained sound that stabbed at me like a knife point.

"Hey!" I kept shouting. "Hey, I'm sorry!—I'll stop pulling." I was saying anything to help myself think.

I heard other, far-off shouts, and a scream, a man's scream, which sounds worse than a woman's, I think, because you don't hear men scream all that much.

I bent low over the man again. "You hurt bad?" I asked, which was another dumb question, but it was all I could think to ask.

"Yes," he grunted. I noticed he was holding both hands tight to his belly. Maybe a big ram caught him square in the gut with a hoof or with its stupid head.

"You need time to get your breath," I said, hoping that was all he'd need.

"No." He shook his head. "I . . ." His head flopped to one side. I slapped his cheek lightly with the back of my hand, but his head wobbled. I wondered if he was dead. His hands loosened and one fell away. I touched his shirt with the back of my fingers. It was wet. I knew it was blood.

I looked toward the burning wagon and I saw men on horses ride back and forth in front of it as if dancing in the flames. I saw another man walking with his hands held behind his head while a man on horseback, I couldn't see who it was, raised a club high, and brought it down on the man, who collapsed.

There were still a fair number of sheep running full bore, but some had turned and were kicking straight back at us, with a couple of riders whooping and pounding hard behind them.

I waved my arm and shouted, but if anybody or any critters heard or saw me, they didn't let on. I had to get this bleeding man away from harm, and figured if he was still alive, he couldn't scream if he was knocked out.

I grabbed hold of his arms again, up high at his pits, and dragged him backward toward the trees. The sheep were closing down on us fast, the riders hard after them, but I was closer to the trees than they were to us, so I legged it. I tripped over something, a chuckhole, likely, and hurried to gain my feet again. I kept on tugging the flopped man and hoped he wasn't dead. That's when I smacked into a tree.

The branches poked me in the back like stiff fingers of someone pointing blame. I bent lower and tugged two or three last feet. I dropped backward once more, angled sideways, on my backside with the man draped over my lap. The flopped man groaned and I sat leaning against the tree, trying to catch my breath. What with the sheep stink and dust and smoke, breathing was none too easy.

"You're okay now," I said. I tried to shove out from under him, but he commenced to moaning, a low, tight sound, so I stopped and sat still. His eyes flicked open and closed, and I held his head between my hands. "You'll be okay soon, mister. My friends are coming. Boss will know what to do."

Even as I said it, I wondered if that was the truth. I gave up trying to figure out who had hurt the man, the sound of the gunshots still fresh in my mind. I leaned back against the tree and heard whoops and sheep bleating and fire roaring and saw sparks snaking upward, too close to trees.

All I wanted was to see Cook, feel his big hand on my shoulder, see his head shaking side to side, telling me I was going to eat the ranch to the poorhouse, the way I packed food into my mouth.

But all I heard was the man in my lap moaning louder and higher up, like he was coming to some decision.

Up rode two horsemen. One of them came real close, and he said, "That's the devil who tried to topple me off my horse! I let him have it." It was Earl. He leaned down. "Dilly, what are you doing with that woolly bastard?"

Earl looked behind himself toward the other rider, and back to me. "Get out from under him, Dilly. I aim to finish off the job. I don't like to leave a task hanging."

The other man rode closer. It was Boss. "Get out of there, Dilly. You go find your horse and ride back to the ranch. Now!"

I don't know to this day how I found the sand to say and do what I did. "No, sir." I shook my head and the man in my lap moaned, long and low. "I will not move and let Earl shoot this man some more. This ain't what you said it was going to be. You said we were going to talk. Persuade the sheepmen is what you said."

Boss let out a long, deep breath. "Hang fire, boy. This is none of your concern. You don't know what you talk of. Too young, never should have let you come along."

"That's a fact," said Earl, not taking his eyes off me.

"Shut your mouth, Earl."

"Yes, sir."

Boss climbed down off his horse and handed the reins up to Earl without looking at him. Earl took them. Boss walked close, bent low over the man, and looked at him. Boss showed his teeth, looking for all the world like he was about to bite the man or me.

When Boss spoke, he growled. "That vile cur," he pointed a thick finger at the man in my lap, "cannot live, Dilly. He will know us and that will not stand. You hear me?"

I heard the anger in his voice shaking his words like dry branches rattling together in a windstorm.

I saw that he could shoot the man without hurting me if that is what he chose to do, by being so close. Elsewise he might shoot both of us, which is something he might consider, too, given what I'd said.

I shoved out from under the man in my lap, who moaned louder as I got to my feet.

"Good boy," said Boss. "Now stand away, go find your horse." He pulled out his pistol.

"I know you, Boss. And you, too, Earl."

Those few words changed my life more than any others I ever spoke.

I stayed standing in front of the sheepman. Boss raised the pistol and aimed it at me. I didn't think he would shoot me, but it's an odd feeling to have a gun pointed at you. Even if it's somebody you know, you can't really be certain.

Earl shouted, "Get out of the way, you fool kid!"

I lunged at Boss, knocked down on his arm hard with mine, and the gun spun out of his hand. I hit Boss's arm harder than I expected, I reckon, because I heard something crack and he howled and collapsed to his knees, holding his arm. I think I broke it. I know my own left arm, halfway to my elbow, didn't like what I'd done to it.

Boss's pistol hit one of the horses in the leg. The horse jumped and Earl shouted some word or other and the two horses, along with a shouting Earl, commenced to bucking and hopping. The horses were already skittish from all the strange commotion of the night, and this didn't help gentle them any.

The whole time, I did my best to stay put in front of the sheepman. What I could do for him, aside from keeping him from getting shot again, I don't know.

"You broke my arm, you worthless whelp! Should have sent you packing when you first turned up! You lousy cur . . ." Boss was on his feet and rummaging for his pistol. I thought I was going to have to rush at him, knock him down. I figured I was in for a penny, as Granna used to say, might as well go whole hog. But he grabbed up the gun and stuffed it into his holster.

Earl had come back, leading Boss's horse behind his own.

"You want help, Boss?"

Boss didn't answer him. He held his broke right arm close to his vest, grabbed the saddle horn with his left hand, and hoisted himself up, groaning and barking blue words due to the pain, or me, or both.

"Boss, we can't leave them . . ."

"Shut up, Earl!"

I won't credit him with much, but Earl shut his mouth. Didn't affect his eyes, though, which he narrowed at me. He shook his head to show me he disapproved of me, and let Boss ride on ahead of him. Boss didn't look back, I know because I watched him ride off, his words still stinging like angry bees.

I looked back in time to see Earl riding hard at me, a few paces from me, swinging an axe handle. I turned away and dove forward, but he caught me down low, across my backside, high on the back of my left leg. It drove me onto my right knee and I fell forward, a couple of feet from the wounded sheepman's boots.

Earl howled laughter as I lay there stunned, feeling as if I'd been trampled and beaten, which I had been. The last I saw or heard of any of them that night was watching Earl's horse pound away into the dark, that axe handle hanging low and swinging as he rode, his laughter carrying over the last of the sheep bleats and screams.

I crawled over to the sheepman, grabbed him by one leg, and gently shook it. "Hey," I said. "Hey, I have a horse somewhere. We'll get Cook. I can ride for him."

As I said it, I knew it was impossible. I would not be welcome at the ranch, not ever. Did that mean I'd never see Cook again? That was the only thing I cared about. I crawled up closer, beside the sheepman, but I knew even before I shook him again that he was dead. He faced the sky, on his back on the ground, one hand still laid across his belly. The other lay in the dirt, palm up, as if waiting for a hand to help him. I put my hand in his, tugged, but his fingers didn't close over mine.

"Hey! You got to wake up!" I shook his shoulder hard and slapped his cheek. "I can help you. Let me find my horse. You'll like him, his name's Monty, that's short for Montgomery. Franklin introduced me and him. Oh, you'd like Franklin, too. He—"

A far-off sound like a man crying, or maybe it was a sheep, came to me. I looked around, but it was dark and the wagon fire had burned down lower. I didn't hear it again.

I looked at the man beside me. He was not much older than me, from what I'd seen of his face earlier. He was dead, though. And that was the last thing he'd ever be.

I laid on my belly beside him, my side and back and leg aching so fierce I thought I might not stand it. But as bad as I felt, I was alive, which was more than he would ever be again.

I fell asleep like that, and the next thing I knew, I heard a horse.

CHAPTER SEVENTEEN

It was Monty I was hearing. I knew it before I even opened my eyes. But not before I felt my whole body ache as if it was a hammer-struck thumb.

I opened one eye, and it hurt, too, especially when the gray light came into it. Then the other eye. But that one saw only blackness. I didn't know what that meant. I thought I'd gone blind in that eye, so I tried to lift my head. Sharp, hot pains buzzed up my shoulder and neck. I rested my head again, waited, then raised it higher, though it hurt like the devil himself was pestering me.

That went on for what felt like a day, and I figured out the trouble. I was laid out facedown. I pushed myself up, felt more hot pains, but kept on going. When I was nearly to my knees, I recalled what had happened the night before. That's when I remembered the young man dead beside me. I turned my head and he wasn't there.

I turned over and looked around, past where he'd been, and saw in the early gray light, through the foggy, misted field before me, white blobs that might have been rocks. I recalled more from the night before. They were sheep, of course, dead sheep, and I had helped kill them, by being there with Boss and Earl and the rest of the boys.

I didn't club any sheep, but I felt as guilty—seeing those white blobs looking more like sheep with every second—as if I'd done the clubbing.

133

Monty broke my spell. He sounded close, but where was he? He nickered again, from behind me in the trees. I got my feet under me, using the tree, and a whole lot of grunting and whining, I don't mind saying, and squinted into the darker patch of trees. "Monty? Where you at?"

He made a low, grumbly sound and I saw him, not twenty feet from me, standing hard by a tree. I shoved away from my leaning tree and, oh, did that first step hurt. The clubbing from Earl came back to me, and if he was there in front of me, I would have jumped at him, stiffness or no. How I ever thought we might be friends was the thinking of a fool. Cook was right, Earl only liked one person and that was himself.

"Hey, boy, hey," I said as I stiff-walked forward, my right arm held out in front of me. I guess he thought I had an apple, because he nudged his head forward. I kept talking low and steady to him like Franklin told me to with horses. It worked, but that also might be because Monty is such a tired-out old fellow. About like I felt that morning.

"Hey, boy, hey," I said, running my hand down his long nose. He smelled like he always does, dust and age and warmth, and bobbed his head like he does when I visit him in the barn or corral. He also poked at my coat for an old snack. But I didn't think to bring him anything before I left the ranch.

The idea that I'd left the ranch and would not be going back stopped my hands patting him. Would I always end up fouled in painful matters?

Monty couldn't reach back to nudge me with his nose like he always does when I pat his neck and shoulders. That's when I saw the reins were tangled tight around two branches. I almost untangled them, but then I saw the saddle had slid down from on top of him so it hung under his big belly.

I figured I'd get that righted around while he was stuck so he couldn't nip at me, because he did that once when I was trying to saddle him. I saw him do that to Franklin once, too, who'd smacked him on the nose for it. I didn't want to do that, as Monty is my friend, and I don't think friends should go around punching on each other. But I wasn't taking any chances, as the night before had been an odd one. Could be he was still worked up.

I also wondered if he was going to go running back to the ranch if I turned him loose. I did not have to worry. By the time I got the saddle slid back up on top of him and the reins untied, he seemed even more tired. We must have made a sorry ol' sight as I led him out of the trees and back to where I'd spent the night facedown in the scrubby, chewed grass.

My left arm was paining me worse than my back and hip, which flared when I walked, but not much else. But my arm . . . yes, there came another recollection of the night before. I'd knocked hard on Boss's arm and did damage to him. I know that for certain. That cracking sound I'd heard had to be his arm.

What was I thinking, attacking the man who'd taken me in and let me live at the ranch? As quick as that thought came to me, the words he'd spit at me stung me all over again.

I held Monty's reins and he commenced to nibbling on whatever grass he could find—those sheep do tend to chaw the grass down to the nub. But Monty was set on the task. It made me smile a little, and I realized he was likely thirsty, too, snagged up all night as he was in the branches. Come to think on it, I was craving a drink myself.

I licked my lips and they were puckered and cracking. It was early, though, and not warm enough to shuck that long duster. I looked it over as I eased back down against that same tree I'd been by all the night before.

The reins bounced in my fingers as Monty moved his nose along the ground. I looked at the churned dirt beside where I was, wondering where the man's body had gone. I didn't see much of a sign of a scuffle in the dirt. What if the whole thing had been something my mind came up with?

That would mean the young man hadn't died of a bullet wound in the belly. That thought gave me hope, as doubtful as it seemed. And once more, my eyes closed when I did not want them to. I guess I was more tired than I thought. I drifted off thinking that the man had been fine after all, and had come to and got up and walked off in the night.

The next time I woke, it was because something was touching me, kicking at my leg. No, not kicks so much as taps. But they were enough to wake me. This time when I opened my eyes it was pure daytime, bright and blue. And cut out of the blue over me was the black shape of a man.

The shape wasn't wearing a hat, and it didn't move. I noticed something odd. The shape's shoulder was bent down as if it was leaning. The shape moved and kicked at me again.

"Hey," said a man's voice.

I knew it was the young man who had died beside me. I am not ashamed to say I tried to get up and let out with a scream at the same time. I hope I did not sound like a baby, but I believe I did. I was backed up against that tree that wouldn't let me go anywhere.

He bent lower, slowly, until his face wasn't but a foot from mine. Now I could see him clearly, since I was no longer looking up at the bright blue sky. It wasn't the dead man. It was an old man. He had dark skin and a wrinkled face, a scruff beard, big ears, and dried blood all along one side of his head. His eyes were wet looking, but not angry.

"Hey," he said again.

He stared at me until I stopped moving. All except for my chest. I was breathing hard like I ran a whole lot, something I am not prone to doing, mostly because it seems silly to get winded out like that. But when you get scared, you get winded without running a single step.

He stood, halfway, and held something toward me with his left hand. I didn't move and he didn't stop staring at me. I looked at the thing. It was a white tin bowl with chips in the finish, a wooden spoon handle sticking out of it. He moved it like he was tired of holding it, and I understood what he meant. He was offering me something to eat.

I tried to stand again, but I was stiff, as before. I groaned and gave up, tried again, and the old man bent lower. It looked like it pained him. He moved the bowl in front of my face. His hand was thick, with bent fingers and big knuckles.

I took it and said, "Thank you."

The old man scuffed backward, and off to my left side a few steps. I could see him better now. Yes, his right shoulder was angled odd. And his right arm was hanging funny, too, swinging as he moved.

He stared at me a long time. The tin bowl was hot, but I didn't move. Finally, he said in a raw, hoarse voice, "I saw what you did."

Oh no, I thought. *He thinks I killed the young man.* "No, no, I didn't—"

He closed his eyes and shook his head slow. He looked as if his whole head hurt. Probably did, because from the looks of him, he'd been through a whole lot worse than me the night before. He held up his left hand. I stopped talking.

"You tried to save him. Thomas."

He stared at me again, not angry, not much of anything. His eyes were watery and red. He had that bad cut on his head but the blood was dried. "What you did, that was good. I am not angry. I am Rafael."

He did not hold out his hand to shake. In my experience when someone tells you their name, they often will hold out a

137

hand. But I guess that isn't always the way it happens. Also, I have not met all that many people who tell me their names. Enough to count on my two hands.

"I . . ." It felt like burrs clogging my throat. I swallowed and tried again. "My name is Dilly." I nodded, by way of avoiding the handshake, not that he was expecting one. He looked to be too pained. I wanted to offer him a seat, but it would be an odd gesture, considering the field was likely his. Or anyways, more his than mine.

What he was telling me gave me pause. I still hadn't touched the spoon, though the top of the soup looked tasty. In truth I could eat the bark off the tree I was leaning against and be satisfied.

I stared again at the ground next to me. He must have understood what that meant, because he said, "He was my nephew. Thomas. The boy you helped."

I looked at him because his voice got funny and quivery. He nodded. He knew what I was going to ask. "Is he . . . did he . . . die?" That word felt like one of the hardest ones I ever had to say. It's a tricky word, something we all will do at some time or other, but not a word I like to think on much.

"Yes." He breathed long and deep, let it out, and he looked even smaller than before. "Yes, he was not able to stay." He looked up to the blue sky. It was a pretty day. He said something in a whisper, but in a language I do not know, which could be one of many since I only know one.

I reckon he was praying. I hadn't imagined it, any of it. All the bad things of the night before. I looked past him out at the meadow. There were dozens of dead sheep all over, as if a giant hand had tossed them like dice from high up in the sky and this was where they landed, no order or reason.

Some of them had their dirty-looking legs poking outward from their puffy bodies, bent in running poses, some looked like they were sleeping, some had red-black stains on their heads and backsides where they'd been beaten with axe handles. Again I felt the cold snake of guilt crawl around and around in a circle in my gut.

I looked at the soup, still warm in my hand, but I didn't feel like eating any more than those sheep had felt like dying. "I am sorry, mister." I couldn't look him in the eye anymore. His eyes hurt too much to look on. I shook my head and my own tears began again. I swear, it's something I must have got from my Granna, or my mother. I'll bet she was a crier. I don't think Big Dilly, my pap, was. But I never really knew him, did I?

"Our home . . ."

I looked up at him, but his eyes weren't on me anymore. I followed to where they were looking. I only saw the dark sticks reaching up into the sky like a stand of blackened grasses or arms raised up, waving for help that never came. It was the wagon. Or what was left of it.

I'd seen sheep wagons before, on my travels, and sneaked into one once when I was passing by the edge of a field where it was setting. The top was a white canvas tarpaulin, but the rest of it was green, and the wheels were a faded red, light though, like longhandles washed too often and left to dry in the sun too many times.

I'd seen the man, a shepherd, leaving the wagon. A black-and-white dog had been sleeping under it that limped after him as he climbed atop a saddled horse and rode away toward a close-up mountain.

I waited a good while and thought on it a while longer. The man, along with the dog, was gone from sight over a long, low rise of green, so I sneaked over a jag of rock and into the field. Without giving myself time to think more on it, I climbed up the narrow wooden steps, one, two, three, and on the fourth I reached for the door. I tugged it open and looked inside. It was light, brighter than a lot of houses I'd been in.

The inside was wonderful. Straight ahead at the far end was a big bed stretching from one side to the other, but it was up in the air, and beneath it were cabinets, and in the center was a table that looked to be slid out from beneath the bed. There was a little wooden stool tucked under the tabletop. On it was a tin cup and a plate and a few other things I didn't take the time to recall.

Closer to me on my right side stood a small woodstove with a pipe that bent up through the wall by the door. On my left was a tall cupboard, lower along were countertops over cupboards. On the floor tucked to the right side were socks and a pair of leather moccasin-looking shoes. Camp shoes, I've heard them called.

I fancied I heard a sound behind me, so I closed the door and jumped down the steps to the ground and over those rocks and back to the road, and I ran and ran and did not look back.

I do not know if that shepherd had returned and was about to shoot me in the back, or if maybe a bear or a wolf or a thousand sheep were about to get me good. But I ran that day for as long as I dared. It took some time for me to turn and look behind me. Nothing but fields of green-and-brown scrubby grass as far as I could see, with the mountains off to the north and a two-rut roadway before and behind me. I stood long enough to get a leg up on my breath, and I loped on. I did not want an angry shepherd to run me down. He would be a-horseback, I reasoned, and I was not. Oh, the things we do when we're spooked.

Since that day I have always admired sheep wagons, as I learned they are called, thinking that they contained all a fellow might need to live a long, quiet time alone, without bother by others. I also have learned to not poke my sniffer in places

Dilly

where it does not belong, which is any place that ain't mine or where I'm not invited in for a snack.

141

Chapter Eighteen

I tasted the soup. It seemed the thing to do. Also, I was hungrier than I can recall being in a long time. About as I always felt before I got to the ranch. The spoon clunking in the bowl made the old man look from the burnt wagon back at me.

I swallowed. "I didn't know you took him. Your nephew, I mean. In the night." I looked at the spot where the young man had lain.

He nodded. "I will bury him not far. On land we own."

I didn't say anything, but I knew this was free range land, and nobody, not even Boss, owned it. It was there for anybody to use, but burying somebody on it? "I thought this land was open range."

I let the idea hang in the cold air between us. He nodded. "Yes, but the land I talk of is my own. It was to be my nephew's land. He would make it a large, fine ranch one day." He looked back toward the smoking wagon. When he looked back at me his eyes were hard, and it seemed as if he were now awake. "You . . . why did you come here with them? Didn't you know?"

He looked angry, old, and sad, and crazy in his head. "Off his bean," as Cook had said about how a man can lose sight of himself if he gets too angry. I didn't understand it when he told me that, but seeing the old sheepman's eyes staring at me, I understood.

I wanted to tell him I thought I could stop Boss by getting folks to talk with each other. I wanted to, but I knew any reason

I offered would sound foolish. His nephew had died because Boss was angry and thought he deserved all the land he could see. And I rode in here with him.

"You cannot stay. This is not a place for a boy. I know this now."

What does a fellow like me do when he hears that? Nothing. I sat there wondering what to do next. I couldn't go back to the ranch, couldn't stay where I was. I could always take to the trail again.

I finished the soup and he gently took the bowl and spoon from me. His thick fingers had hard, shiny nails like small river stones. A working man's fingers.

"Thank you kindly," I said, nodding. "That was the best soup I ever ate."

That might have been a stretch, but I wanted about ten more bowls full. He nodded and walked back toward the smoldering wagon. It looked like a picked-over chicken carcass. It must have pained him something awful to look at the mess left to him.

I saw more about me as the sun rose, more live sheep nibbling grass. Must have been about a hundred of them all mixed in with the dead ones. There were lots of dead sheep, too, like white rocks. Did this old man think I was nothing more than a murdering cowboy? He fed me soup, that had to mean something.

He surely needed help, so why was he in such a hurry to get rid of me? I figured I'd keep out of his way, but I had to help him clean up this mess. Besides, whenever I woke up stiff and sore, I knew I needed to get moving.

It took me some minutes before I could walk without looking older than the old man. I didn't dare peek under my clothes for fear I'd see bruises the likes of which don't show up on living people. Monty was still behind me eating grass. I wished I had a

143

longer rope so he could stray further, but I didn't dare turn him loose. He'd like as not make his way back to the ranch, and where would I be? As I was when I showed up there.

I leaned against him and smoothed my hand along his neck and shoulder. I liked the way he smelled. I liked his pretty brown eyes and the shiny, smooth hair on his neck, and the little bumps here and there that told me horses are no different than people. None of us is smooth, we all have puckers and scars and welts and whatnots from everyday living.

Monty was old, older than me. That's why he wasn't wanted around the ranch. I felt sure we deserved to be together, but he wasn't my horse. He belonged to Boss. So I guess if I left with him, that would make me a horse thief. Way Boss was, I don't think he'd forget I was riding Monty. Maybe he'd think the horse ran off in the fracas? I decided I'd leave it alone for the time being and keep Monty with me.

I heard a noise from southward, up the same path through the trees we'd taken the night before. Sounded like a horse. Monty heard it, too, because he stopped nibbling grass and perked his ears in the same direction as his eyes. He gave a low, bouncy sound.

A dark shape rose up and grew bigger as the horse approached up the rise. I leaned to my right for a better look. I moved closer to the tree I'd been leaning against.

Pretty soon the dark thing was a hat on top of a head on top of a big body on top of a horse. And then it was Cook. I didn't recognize him at first because I'd never seen Cook riding a horse. I never saw him leave the ranch, for that matter. I wanted to run and shout hello to him, but I didn't think the old sheepman would take to a happy-sounding ruckus.

"Dilly!"

I could tell by the way he said it he wasn't angry. Well, a little. Mostly he sounded and looked relieved. Me, too. It was nice to see someone I knew. I wondered if he was going to try to take me back to the Hatterson.

He rode up, keeping his gaze on me. He only broke it to climb down, because he's a big fellow and has to watch where he's putting his feet, I guess. He looked at me again as he walked forward. "Dilly," he repeated, but this time he sounded satisfied, like he'd solved a tricky riddle.

"Hi, Cook," I said, knowing he must be steamed with me for running off the night before.

"I see Boss wasn't lying."

I didn't say anything.

"Yeah," he continued. "He's not too happy with you. Boy, you stoved up that arm of his in good shape. I figure a bone inside's cracked. He's a tough man, but his face was gray from the pain and he was holding it funny. Wanted me to help him with it, but I said I wouldn't until he told me what happened to you. Boss said, 'Oh, that kid didn't come to no harm.' I know Boss a long ol' time, and he will get up to a lot of things, but he wouldn't lie to me. So I came on my own to see. I would have been here sooner, but I had to help patch up the other men. I set off, but I got turned around. Lost hours wandering around up here. Serves me right for not exploring these hills more when I had my days off. Too lazy, by half."

Cook is not a lazy man, and I was about to say so when he looked away. "I'm sorry, Dilly. I should have been here sooner." He looked back at me. "You okay? I mean it, now. Don't lie to Cook."

I nodded. "Yes, sir. I'm feeling fine."

"You don't look fine, Dilly. You look stiff. I can tell by how you're standing. Usually you move around like you have a trouser full of snakes."

"Oh, I . . . I fell off Monty is all."

"Uh-huh."

He didn't believe me, but he didn't make any more fuss over it. He looked past me. I turned and saw the old man back by his wagon, bent over tugging on a dead sheep.

"Oh, now, what has Boss done here? This is no good, no good at all. I don't care if the sheep folks are here illegal, legal, or passing through. There's no call for this." He looked at me again. "You going to tell me what happened here last night, Dilly?"

From all the dead sheep and the burned-out wagon, I thought it was kind of obvious, but I shrugged.

"Boss and the boys, they didn't end up talking like you hoped, huh?"

"No, sir." I couldn't look at him. I knew he was about to make fun of me and if I looked at him I might start blubbering, and I felt old, far too old to commence crying every time something lousy happened in my life.

"One of the men, Manny it was, said he thought a sheepman had been shot. That true?"

I didn't say anything, felt my face heat up.

"Dilly." Cook moved closer, pushing my face up under my chin so I was looking at him. "Did they shoot someone?"

I nodded, and started crying. I guess I was not old enough to stop with all that. Maybe it's okay now and again. It felt like I had been waiting for Cook to come along so I could cry myself out again. He hugged me like he did after Earl beat on me, patting my head with one of his big hands. I kept thinking how those hands are the same ones that could peel a potato with that big knife of his and make all the peel come off in one long, curly tail.

"Is the shot-up man dead, Dilly?"

I nodded and didn't pull my face away from his chest. He still smelled of coffee and sweat and beans and bread and tobacco and . . . Cook.

He sighed. "Oh, my."

He pushed me away from him gently and led me over to his horse. "Rummage in there, I brought biscuits and the fixings for more, plus beans and coffee. Few other things. And some of those dried apple slices I know Monty likes."

I looked at him with wide eyes. How did he know?

"You think you and Franklin can get anything by ol' Cook? I keep a sharp eye on everything in my stores." He smiled and nodded toward the old sheepman. "That man yonder, he bother you at all?"

I shook my head. "He fed me. Soup."

"Oh?"

I nodded and told him what had happened, how I held the young man, who it turns out was the old man's nephew, and woke up to find he was gone. I told him what the old man told me, about owning his own land, and how he wasn't angry with me. Or if he was, he was pretty good at hiding it. I left out the part where Earl bashed on me with the axe handle. I didn't want Cook to go back to the ranch and beat Earl to death, which I kind of figured he might do. Cook would be in worse trouble than anyone in this whole mess.

"Okay," said Cook, when I was done. "I aim to talk with him."

And he did. Left me with his horse, which I tied to a tree near Monty, but not so close they'd tangle. I set to work on those biscuits, all the while keeping my own sharp eye on Cook and the old man. They were standing and talking. Cook bent low and helped the man move the dead sheep he'd been tugging on. He did the same with a few more. From the way he kept turning his head and nodding, I could tell they were still talking.

Cook walked back after a while and I chewed faster the closer he got so my mouth wouldn't be full of biscuit, but it was.

They're awfully good but they're dry work. I should have taken a pull on the canteen.

"Last night, we had an argument, me and the boss. After I rigged up his arm." He shook his head. "Accused me—me!—of being a traitor, of siding with your friend there." Cook nodded once toward the burned wagon.

"It's my fault," I said, looking at my boots. I felt lower than I had in a long time.

"No, it ain't, neither, Dilly. It's been a long time coming. Took something to make it happen. That part I can blame on you. But that's good, you see. You got me to make a change that needed making for some time now. Too bad we all didn't take Franklin's advice and get out before everybody and their brother turned ornery."

"That wouldn't have helped the sheepmen, though."

Cook looked at me as if I'd started barking like a dog. He nodded. "You're right, Dilly. You do surprise me, boy. I tell you that. Anyway, I come to take you with me."

"But you said you and Boss had an argument."

"That I did. Doesn't mean I'm not going back to the ranch. But not for long, you see. I am set to make my way to Spokane, Washington. There's a logging operation out that way, that my sister told me in a letter is going gangbusters. I reckon one of those log camps will need a camp cook. Wouldn't be much different than a ranch, I don't expect. Besides, it's been years since I've seen Martha, that's my sister. Be nice to see her again, before it's too late."

"Too late for what?"

"Life, Dilly. Life. The most precious thing we all own, and most of us bumble through our days as if there were lots of them before us. Truth is, each day that comes, there's one less day left open to us. You understand?"

"Yes, sir," I said, though in truth I wasn't certain. I was still too sore, but I'd think on it later.

"Okay. Get Monty righted around. You come on with me." He looked around. "This ain't no place for you, Dilly."

He sounded like the old man. "He's a nice man," I said.

"Yes, I reckon he is. He's full of grief, I know that. No telling what he'll be like once that passes."

"I think he'll still be nice, Cook."

He nodded as he watched the old man shuffling near the black wagon.

"I'm surprised he is," I said. "What with having to put up with Boss and the boys raiding them all the time. That would put me in a bad mood."

Cook chuckled. "Tell me about it, Dilly. I been putting up with that man for a dozen years. Time to move on, I say. And it's time for you to come with me."

I cleared my throat. "I can't do it, Cook."

"Why not?"

"He needs me."

Cook looked at me, but different now, as if he didn't know me anymore. Finally, he rubbed a big hand on his whiskery face and blew out air. "I figured you'd say that, but I had to try." He pointed to the packed place beneath the tree where I'd spent the night. "If that's the way it's going to be, this spot's as good as any."

"For what?" I said.

"For your camp, boy. You have to set yourself up so you can get sleep and eat. The old man will be up by his wagon, what's left of it, anyway. But he has a heap of work to do here. He'll also need help burying his nephew. Said his land isn't all that far. Got a pile of sheep that need tending. He wants to skin out a couple. The rest will commence to spoil once the day's heat starts. I expect he'll want the green hides to tan. He'll show you what you need to know."

149

He waved a big hand at the field of dead sheep, and shook his head. "Ain't right, ain't right at all. I should have listened to you, boy. You taught me a good lesson."

I didn't know what to think. I never thought I could teach a man like Cook anything at all. I looked at him, must be my eyes were wide because he said, "You up for this, Dilly? You told me you thought he'd need your help."

"Yes, sir." I nodded.

"Okay. After today, I'll be back as I can, now that I know the way."

"But when are you going to Spokane, to the logging camp?"

"Not yet. Me and Boss, we argued, sure, but he's no fool. He knows a ranch runs on its belly. He'd have to be more steamed up than he is to cut me loose. Besides, I know things." He winked and tapped the side of his nose.

"What's that mean?" I said. "About Boss?"

"You never mind. Teach me to keep my mouth open and words falling out." He shook his head at himself. "But I reckon things will simmer because the law, which has been in Boss's back pocket for far too long, has been feeling a pinch from folks who don't like what's happening to the sheepherders. Seems these woollies and their tenders bring in money to the town. A whole lot of money. Money that folks don't want to lose out on because of a few hot-headed ranchers who already have plenty of their own land, anyway."

"So this is all about money," I said.

"Always is, Dilly. From sunup to sundown, that's what makes us all do whatever it is we do in a day's time."

"I don't want to be like that, Cook."

"That's up to you to figure out, Dilly. You do, you let me know, okay?"

I nodded.

"Your old man yonder," he gestured with his head toward the

old man standing crooked before the smoldering wagon. "He's going to need help burying his kin. You up to the task?"

"I am." In truth, I was scared. I'd never helped bury anybody before, but like everything, there was always a first time.

"Good. He told me he's going to take him to his own land. Man's a genuine landowner thataway." He pointed toward what I think was northeast. "Past that valley and ridge beyond. It's where the free range land peters out. Some private parcels out that way."

"How do we get him there?"

"I offered to help, but he says he has a mule somewhere hereabouts. I think he's proud. But you have Monty, so I told him to bundle up the boy. He has tarpaulin, and ol' Monty would carry him. You go along, too. It'll take most of the day. He'll have to leave his sheep, but I'll make sure Boss and the boys don't make a return visit."

"You think they will?" That notion hadn't come to me yet, but now that Cook said it, I knew it would be all I'd think about.

"Nah," he said. "I think they're too tired, and between you and me, I think they're ashamed. Most of them, anyway."

He smacked his big hands together. "I'll bring you more food, don't worry. And I'll do what I can at the ranch to get the boys to come around to the smart way of thinking about all this. The law in Greenhaven, too. They need to know a man has been killed. That should make a difference."

He mounted up. "Shouldn't take much to convince the boys they're on the wrong side of this thing," he said. "After last night, most of them were bothered, I could tell. Except Earl. He's an idiot."

I had to smile at that.

CHAPTER NINETEEN

Cook was right about the old man wanting to bury his nephew on his own land. And what's more, even though I doubted it when he told me, the old man did own land.

I guess Cook talked to him about using Monty, because I led that horse over to where the old man had laid out his nephew, though now the young man was wrapped in a tarpaulin and lashed around tight with a rope. I set down a sack of food, mostly biscuits, and a canteen, both of which Cook had left with me.

I had cinched up Monty's saddle and did my best to make him look smart, but the old man said nothing, so I stood there, not sure what to do next.

He didn't ask for help at all. Normally I would respect that in a man, but he had only one arm that was of use, and his head was still bloodied, though he had washed himself a little from the creek that ran along the northern edge of the meadow.

He bent over his nephew and tried to hoist him up. I bent low and grabbed hold of the dead man's shoulders, but the old man looked at me and said, "No."

I lowered the dead man to the ground, but didn't move away. The old man grunted and strained and tried, but there was no way in a month or a year that he was going to lift that body with one arm and lay him across the saddle.

Still bent over the boy, with sweat dribbling off his nose, the old man said, "Okay." But he didn't look up.

I lifted the young man, who was smaller than me, but somehow felt twice as heavy. I managed to get him up onto my shoulder, and I knew his head was facing my back, his bloody waist bent over my shoulder.

Pained as I was from my trampling and beating of the night before, I hardly felt it because all I kept thinking was that I was carrying a dead man. I was glad of the tarpaulin. Somehow it helped me in my head to know I had something between me and him.

Monty sidestepped a little but held, and it wasn't until I got the young man lifted up and across the saddle, facedown, that I saw the old man had steadied the horse. We used a second rope to tie around the dead man's shoulders and head, and passed it beneath Monty. I tried to keep it aligned with the cinch so it wouldn't rub Monty on the trip, and made myself promise to check it as we traveled.

Once the body was lashed down, I walked to Monty's head and stroked his nose and gave him a slice of dried apple. He didn't seem too bothered by having a dead man on his back, no more than I was, I reckon. I held the reins.

"Which way?" I said, but the old man put his hands on the reins above mine.

"No, you stay here, with the sheep." He looked frightened, as if what Cook said, about the men coming back, might happen any minute. I didn't know what to think.

"You going to be able to dig . . . well, a grave on your own? With your arm hurt and all, I mean."

The old man turned his bloodshot brown eyes from me and looked out across the ridge toward where I thought we were going, if Cook was right. He let out a breath as if he was tired and only wanted to sleep, and said, "Okay. But the sheep will be left alone."

He looked past me toward the sheep. Those still alive had

crowded down toward the far end of the meadow and appeared to be doing the only thing I've ever seen sheep do, at least up until last night, anyway. They were eating grass.

But there was nothing for it, he knew it and I knew it. I reckon even ol' Monty knew it. If he wanted his nephew buried on his own land, the old man needed me along to dig the grave. He handed me the reins, picked up a shovel, and walked ahead of me. I settled the food sack on my shoulder, looped the canteen on my other shoulder—I figured Monty had enough work to do hauling that poor dead man—and we followed along.

It took us much of the day, stopping every hour or so to rest. We moved at a steady walk, mostly because the old man couldn't or wouldn't move faster. At a certain point, still some hours before dark, Rafael stopped and nodded. "We have arrived at my land."

I looked around. It was the same as the land we'd passed through—scrubby trees and long, dried-out grasses moving in a welcome breeze. I wondered how he could tell where he was. He began walking again and kept on going. We angled down a wash that led to a creek, up a long, low, grassy slope that leveled off at the top. Trees, ponderosa pines, I think, grew here and there. Once we got through them, we stepped out onto a pretty meadow about like where we'd left the sheep. But this one had a pile of something covered over with three or four torn tarpaulins.

As if he had heard what I was thinking, Rafael said, "Those are logs and boards we have been stacking for building our house. We were to begin building it soon." He shook his head as he stared at the pile and began walking again. We crossed the meadow at the east end, and he stopped again atop a rise.

"Here," he said. "This is a pretty spot for Thomas to spend his days." He looked at me. I nodded, unsure if that's what he was after.

I began untying the boy's body, and slid him off and into my arms, as if I were carrying a baby. He was still loose, not like I'd heard bodies become, stiff like lengths of wood. I laid him gently close to where the old man had sunk the shovel. I went back to Monty and stripped off the bridle and saddle and used the blanket to rub his back.

He liked that, sweaty and tired as I knew he was. He'd had a drink at the creek a few minutes before, so I gave him another apple slice, and with the rope we'd used to lash the body onto him, I tethered him to a tree, long enough that he could graze.

I gently took the shovel from the old man. I made a few scratches in the dry ground, looking up at him as I did to see him nodding. With the size of the hole marked out, I commenced digging.

Sweating has never been my favorite undertaking, but I figure tasks that make you sweat are best to plow through because thinking about them is usually more work than doing them. Once I got the thin soil cuffed off the top, that hole was slow going. But I got it done in a couple of hours.

The old man would wander off without a sound—I reckon I made enough in grunts and gasps for us both. He'd reappear and look down at my progress. He'd also surprise me by dangling the canteen in front of my face so that I'd spook and step back. I think he grew to like doing that to me, though I didn't see a smile on his face.

The service was short. We lowered the young man into the ground. The old man took off his hat and scooped up a handful of gravel and tossed it in the hole. I'm not certain why people do that, but they do. I did the same when he glanced at me.

He said something, sounded like a poem or a prayer, in his language, and crossed himself. I don't know how to do that, not certain if I ever did, but he didn't look at me that time. He stepped back and held his hat in his hands and looked down at his boots, and I saw a tear run a trail down his wrinkly brown cheek. He stayed that way for a long time, so I didn't move. He looked at me and said, "Okay." And turned away.

I took that to mean I could fill in Thomas's grave. So I did, but what an odd feeling that gave me. I was burying a person, a young man who had died while I held him. It was powerful, and I think I might have had some tears of my own mixing with my sweat.

Filling the hole went quicker than emptying it. Even so, we were closing in on dark in a few hours. Rafael must have read my mind, because after I drank from the canteen and ate a biscuit or two, he said, "It is late and you are tired. We will stay here tonight."

I could tell part of him wanted to, so as to not leave his nephew alone, I think, on his first night being buried and all. But leaving the sheep unattended bothered him worse.

"If you'd like, I can go back tonight and see to the sheep, and you can ride Monty back tomorrow, or whenever you have a mind to."

He stared at me. "Thank you." He breathed deep. "We will go together in the morning. What will be, will be, eh?"

I was relieved to hear that, seeing as how I was more tired than I wanted to admit. And I figured we'd spend the last half of the walk in darkness. I was worried about the sheep, too, though. I hoped if coyotes or wolves came around, they'd gnaw on the dead ones first.

CHAPTER TWENTY

Three days in, me and Rafael stopped for a few minutes to catch a breath and drink from the dipper in the leaky wooden bucket before it dripped itself away and dried out again. I wished we had a better bucket because I'm the one who had to fill it from the creek.

It took that many days for him to warm up to me, though I can't say that's the best word for it. He didn't speak much, and regarded me with a curious stare. I reckon he liked the help, though.

After we drank, we were both facing the treeline to the north, with the remnants of Rafael's flock grazing to our west, down the length of the pasture, away from the east-end stink of the carcass pile.

I heard a crunching, snapping sound and got to my feet. I had no gun, but I had found the axe handle I'd let go of that night, and I grabbed it up while we waited, quiet, for whatever might be coming towards us from those trees. It was shaded back in there, and for a few seconds I saw nothing, then black shadows moved. They pulled together into one big shadow that crunched pine branches and became a man I'd never seen on a small spotted horse.

He rode closer and I looked toward Rafael. He relaxed his shoulders—well, the one that hadn't been broken—so I figured the stranger was someone he knew.

The man was younger than Rafael, though his skin was the

same darkish color. He wore a brimmed hat, and his clothes were better than Rafael's. He rode up close, glanced at me, and looked at the old man. He said something in their tongue.

The old man nodded.

"Thomas?"

The old man looked down, as if he were studying an animal track in the dirt.

The man on the horse dipped his head low, leaned forward. "Thomas? Dead?"

The old man slowly shook his head and said in English, "We buried him. He will spend forever on his own land."

The man on the horse slid out of the saddle. "No, no, no!" He shook his head and walked closer to the old man, the reins in his right hand. With his left he pulled off his hat and curled the brim tight in his fingers. If it were made of wood, it would have snapped apart. He stared at Rafael for a full minute as if expecting him to say more. He looked at me, but spoke to the old man.

I imagine he asked who I was.

"This is Dilly," Rafael said in English. "He has come to help me. He is a good boy." As if to prove it, Rafael patted my shoulder.

I was surprised. It was about the most he'd said all at once since the attack. Even though it was a sad time, I felt good about what he said, but it was a waste of effort. The new man stared at me with anger behind those wet eyes. He looked back to the old man.

If he was going to speak, Rafael beat him to it. "Have you seen Pip?"

Him saying this in English took the younger man by surprise. He replied, also in English. "Your dog? No. How long?"

"Since that night, three days now."

The man shrugged. "What happened to your shoulder?" He

had finally noticed Rafael's injury.

They talked for near ten minutes, once more in their own lingo, before shaking hands. Once up on his horse again, the stranger gave me another long look and rode back through the trees.

The old man returned to work. I was already at it, tying a rope to the last of the carcasses. I was about to fetch Monty to drag them when the old man spoke. "That was Ernesto. He is a good man. He is angry with the ranchers, the cattlemen. They did this to him some weeks ago. I told him he should fetch the law. He says he tried, but they are no help."

"I'm sorry. About it all."

The old man shrugged. "It is not your fight to be sorry about. You had a choice and you made good of it. He lost most of his sheep, but he has found about seventy-five that he will bring here. He says if the cattlemen attack again, we will all be together."

I had not put much thought into another attack by the cattlemen. I guess I hoped if I didn't think about it, it might not happen. But I know that's foolish thinking. Mad as Boss was, still would be, I reckon, he would be back.

I hoped Cook could talk sense into the boys. Well, except for Earl. I didn't think anybody could ever talk sense into him. He was mean to the bone.

"Where do you think your dog got to?" I said, knowing a dog would be useful in guarding against wolves and coyotes and bears and mountain lions.

He kept walking away from me and shrugged.

What did that mean?

"I have not seen her since that night."

"What was her name? I can go look for her."

"She was called Pip. But she was old. I think if she was hurt, she is dead. I have looked. She would not have gone far." He shrugged. "I don't know."

I always was afraid of dogs because the ones I'd known were mean, like the big, droopy-cheeked one that the Torbenhasts kept tied outside, at the corner of the barn. It barked and snapped its big white teeth at me whenever I walked near it, which I had to do often in order to get to the dung heap with the wheelbarrow. Still, I felt bad for it when the cold weather came. It was tied out there all the time.

I never saw the Torbenhasts go near it except for once when it barked at something in the woods. Mr. Torbenhast stopped a moment from telling me how to reset the fence post I was sinking and looked to the woods. I did, too, but I didn't dare stop working. He always knew if I slowed my pace, even to wipe sweat from my eyes.

Mr. Torbenhast squinted at the woods while the dog barked, but didn't see anything, so he walked over, his hands still on his waist, and kicked that dog in the chest. The dog, big as he was, yowled and yelped about like I used to when Mr. Torbenhast kicked or punched me. That was when I took a liking to the dog.

I had thought for a long time how I would untie that dog some night, and me and him would run up into the hills and go away together. Find a nice place to live far away from people. But he scared me too much, nearly as much as Mr. Torbenhast scared me.

Once when the family was gone and left me behind, I tried to talk with the dog, but he lunged at me. I let him be for fear that if the chain freed up from where it was nailed to the corner of the barn, he would have at my throat and I would die right there on that farm. What a horrible thought.

That dog was some old, I reckon, but it never knew freedom. It died on a cold night in winter the year before I finally took my leave of the place.

But what if a dog was as kind as Cook? I didn't see any reason why it couldn't be. And what if it was lost and hurt? The thought of that made me want to find Rafael's dog.

The old man didn't care what I did one way or another. I expect it was the grief getting to him. I tried to keep myself quiet and do what needed doing before he got to thinking how he was going to have to do it. I still felt bad about the attack and being part of it. But the old man had said nice things about me to his friend, so that was something.

I figured to repay him by finding his dog. Might make him feel better. It never occurred to me how he'd feel if I should find the dog dead. But that's what happened.

Chapter Twenty-One

I found her in a gulley, close by a tree, far enough from the pasture that we never noticed. She was stretched long like she was sleeping. In fact, I thought at first she was, until I saw the flies lift off her black, blood-matted head and I knew she'd been clubbed like the sheep.

She had short, black-and-white hair with brown speckles along her legs and face. She also had a tuft of yellowish-brown hair along the top of her tail. She was an old dog, I could tell. Wide and thick, but she didn't look mean at all.

"She was my friend. I knew her better than I knew my nephew." Rafael sighed and rubbed his stubbly chin with his good hand.

"He was a good boy. I will have to tell his parents. My sister and her husband. My grief is for them. I will mail a letter, but I cannot leave my flock. They are all I have now that my old mule, Lucky, is gone, and now Pip has been taken from me." We stood quietly looking down at the dead dog.

"Thank you for finding her, Dilly. You are a good boy. I knew her a long time. Longer than I know most people. Longer than I knew my wife and daughter."

A wife and daughter. Where were they? Did he leave them back in his old country, like so many folks I heard about on my own travels? Could be he was looking to get himself a stake, and send for them.

It wasn't until Cook explained it to me that I understood it was not the sort you cut off a big beef critter and eat, but a wad of money or land or something of value that you can make into a life. I figured that was it, that Rafael would send for his wife and daughter, as soon as I could help him round up his missing sheep and build a cabin so they would have a place to live. Simple as that.

Again, there was nothing I could say to all this. I left him standing over Pip and walked fast the short distance to his camp. I tore a small piece of tarpaulin from a ragged, flappy hunk he had set beside his few other saved possessions. I brought it back to them and laid it over Pip, except for her face.

I tapped Rafael on the shoulder. I knew he had seen me doing this, but he still looked at the dead dog with surprise. He looked more hurt than when he had talked about his dead nephew.

He bent to her and with an old, knobby hand, he smoothed the hair on her face.

"Would it be okay to bury her where she is?" I hoped he said yes, because she smelled ripe and I didn't want to haul her too far. I would if he said so.

He said nothing for a time, and finally nodded. A tear pushed out of his eye corner, down his long nose, and dangled there like a raindrop, for a long time.

I turned away.

Like so much Rafael did, he surprised me by talking that night of his family. "Rosa and Lucy, they were my wife and daughter."

He sipped his soup and closed his eyes. While he swallowed, I watched the knobby Adam's apple in his thin neck work up and down like somebody nodding on a deal.

"They became ill from a winter sickness many years ago. My wife was new to me, though I think we loved each other. I can't be certain." He almost laughed but made a small "hmmph" sound. "I don't even remember her face. But I know she was very pretty." He looked at me when he said this, as if I were going to argue with him.

I nodded and didn't say a thing.

"The baby girl, Lucy, if she had lived, she would have been prettier than her mother, which is something to be proud of." He watched the low fire for a while. "It no longer matters. But Pip, I knew that dog for many, many years. And now I will never see her again. This makes me sad and tired."

He sighed and sipped his coffee. I didn't think he was going to say anything else, but he surprised me again.

"I am too old for all this. I should let the cattlemen have what they want. But I promised I would help make this a good place for the Basques to settle, to work for ourselves. That is admirable." He nodded his head and looked at me.

"It began well enough, but the angry cattlemen, like the one you call 'Boss,' came sniffing around. I do not understand. There is enough space for everyone. This country is very big. Big enough for us to all live as friends. I have come to learn not everyone wants this."

CHAPTER TWENTY-TWO

In that first week, I worked like I had never worked before. Harder than any two men. But I couldn't say much, because as sore and as sad as he was, that old man worked beside me the whole day long.

We worked at skinning out the dead sheep. Rafael taught me how. We slit them along the back legs, up the belly, out to the front legs, and peeled that back a little until we got enough to tie a rope onto. We staked the front legs to the ground, and with Monty, pulled the skins backward off the meat. It worked slick, but it was a gruesome, foul job.

We laid the skins out in the sun to cure. It was smelly, bloody work. The blowflies were the worst of it, though. They bite and swarm and you can't wave them away without thinking about it because you're holding a sharp knife. With my luck I'd slice off my nose or ears trying to keep the flies from pestering me.

It took some time, but I learned a little more about him and his family. They're of a people called Basques. He had to spell it for me. He comes from Spain, that's all the way over past England someplace. He drew a map for me in a patch of dirt near where the wagon used to be. I was never much of a hand with maps, so I nodded.

By the time the fire had burned out on the night of the attack, there wasn't much left of the sheep wagon. One of the wheels was pretty good, but only the steel rims of the others were useful. Rafael said he didn't have the money to fix up

165

another wagon, but it didn't matter because he owned land. All he needed to do, he said, was build a house. When he told me that, he looked almost excited for a few seconds. I think he remembered his nephew because his face sagged and got old again.

I asked him why he was using that free range land, and he said because it was his custom to move the sheep around to various grazing grounds.

For the first week or so I jumped at every sound, no matter if it was a sheep yammering—they do like to talk—or Monty crashing around in the trees where he'd go to lean against the bigger ones and scratch himself.

Rafael gave me a length of rope to keep that old horse from straying too far. I tied him to trees for a few days, moving him whenever he chewed away all the grass around them. I tied the rope to a rock and moved it every few hours. That seemed to keep ol' Monty happy.

I was still worried that even if Boss and the boys didn't come back to attack the sheep again, they were likely going to send a lawman after me for horse thieving. But they never did. I figured I'd ask Cook about it when he visited next. I also decided I would send Monty back to the ranch with him.

At the end of that first week, Cook visited again. He brought more biscuits and a good many sacks of fixings for me and Rafael. A sack of coffee, two sacks of flour, cornmeal, and a big sack of beans. He even remembered a double handful of dried apple slices for Monty.

When I asked him if Boss thought I was a horse thief, Cook shook his head. "Boss don't know where that beast has gone. Nobody's mentioned him. I bet they think that ol' horse has wandered off into the mountains to live with the wolves and bears."

Cook and Rafael talked together while I rummaged in the

biscuit bag. When I had one in each hand and a mouthful of another, Cook said, "Dilly. Pull your head out of the feedbag and come over here. I got something to tell you both, and I only want to tell it once."

I did, feeling my ears burn. I offered them each a biscuit, but neither accepted. More for me.

Cook commenced speaking. "Yesterday, Sheriff Barton, from Greenhaven, along with two deputies, rode out to the Hatterson."

That paused my chewing. Rafael, he didn't look much different than he ever does, but he didn't take his eyes from Cook's.

"The sheriff, he's a bigmouth and a blowhard, so what he said didn't much surprise me. In front of the noon crowd loafing in the shade on the porch of the cookshack, Boss there with them, he says, 'Good day, boys. I come here on official business. Seems one of those muttonheads up yonder in the hills has got it in mind that he's been attacked by a band of rowdies. Says they laid low a passel of his sheep and even claims one of their number was killed. I'm talking about a man, not a sheep, now, though you'd be hard-pressed to tell the difference, right? Right?' "

Cook shook his head. "That brought a few laughs from the boys on the porch, though not what you'd expect. The sheriff said, 'So as I say, this is an official visit.' He leaned way over his saddle horn and said, 'If any of you boys hear of somebody committing such foul deeds in my county, why, I hope I don't need to remind you it's your sworn duty as a citizen of this fair land of ours to ride straight to town and look me up. Me and the boys here will look into it. You hear me?' "

Cook rolled his eyes. "The sheriff, he might have said what needed saying, but not in the way it should have been said, you see what I mean, Dilly?"

"I think so. You're saying he's not going to do anything about it, is he?"

Cook shrugged. "Not my place to predict a man's behavior, certainly not a lawman's, but I'd say you're right, if I was a betting man, and I'm not—and don't you never waste your money betting either, you hear me, Dilly?"

He poked a finger at me and this time I nodded. I wasn't exactly certain what betting involved, anyway. I thought it had something to do with playing cards and fancy ladies in saloons. Both of them scared me, so nodding seemed the safest thing to do when Cook looked like that.

I can't be certain, but I think I saw a quick grin slide off Rafael's face. Nah, he never smiled.

"Okay. The other thing that makes me say that is the sheriff and Boss, they went up to the big house, laughing and slapping each other's backs like they were long-lost brothers. They stayed up there a good, long while, no doubt smoking cigars and drinking whiskey. Once in a while you could hear big rounds of laughs coming out those windows of Boss's office."

He shook his head again and said, "I don't know. Might be worth getting some other lawman interested. This can't go unpunished." He looked up at Rafael. "How you feel about me talking with the folks in Greenhaven? I bet that newsman would find this of interest."

I thought it was a great idea, but Rafael rubbed his neck. "I . . . I don't think the people in town are any different than the ones at the ranches."

"Well now, I don't know about that. I been hearing that you sheepmen are doing something the merchants in town like a whole lot."

"Oh?" said Rafael.

Cook nodded. "Yeah, you're spending money, and the more of you folks who come here, the more money you're bringing in. You do enough of that and the only sounds they'll want to hear are coins clinking in their sweaty hands."

"Ah, yes." Rafael nodded. "Money, it's always the money. But for me, it's more important to have a place where my family and friends can settle and call home. You see?"

He said this to Cook, I think, but he looked at me first. I nodded. And I meant it, I really did understand what he was talking about. I understood it before, but at that moment, I really did. The man wanted a home, plain and simple. That's the one thing I always wanted, too.

"I been working on the boys, too," said Cook, looking mostly at me. "Most of them have asked about you. I let on as how you're okay, but I make sure they know I'm disappointed in them all. I told them you're more of a man than any of them together would ever be."

I thought for a second he was funning me, but there wasn't no hint of a grin on Cook's face when he said it. A level stare. I never blushed as hard as I did at that moment. I couldn't even look at Cook. He patted me on the shoulder and said, "Don't let it go to your head, boy. Praise from Cook won't even buy you a slice of pie in town."

I looked at him. "I don't want a slice of pie, Cook. Thanks." It's not exactly what I meant to say, but I think he knows I appreciated his kind words.

We chatted more about this and that, and before Cook mounted up, he pulled out a six-gun and a box of cartridges and handed them to Rafael. "I hope you'll not need this."

Rafael took the gun and nodded his thanks.

Before he left, Cook told me not to worry so much about Monty or the boys. So I tried not to, but that's not so easy to do. I figured there was plenty to worry about. But I trusted that Cook would somehow convince the boys, some of them, anyway, to convince Boss of the error of his ways. Or at least go to town and persuade the folks there that the sheep ranchers were as welcome as anyone else.

As far as worrying about Monty, I was too busy most of the time to pay him much attention. He didn't seem to care. We used him, though. And I was glad for it. And I think he liked it, to be honest. I think being stuck in the barn and the corral, he missed regular cowboy work.

The boys had scared off Rafael's mule and he thought they either stole it or it had died. But the day after Cook visited, a mule turned up. "Is that your mule?" I said, nodding toward the thing that had come dragging into the field. It was a bone rack, all scratched up and flop-eared, but it was a mule. I hoped it was able-bodied enough to help with lugging the dead sheep.

Rafael nodded, and acted like he always did at whatever new thing might be happening, but I could tell by his eyes that he was happy to see that old mule.

I thought Rafael was old, but that mule, Lucky, he called it, was some old. I think it was supposed to be a funny name. And that's true, as that mule was like a four-legged circus clown. Or at least funny like I've heard clowns can be. I have not seen a circus, but I would like to one of these days. He was always falling asleep while I was rigging up a rope on him or watching the buzzards circling above us.

Mostly the mule was friendly, in a quiet way. Come to think on it, he wasn't so different than Monty and Rafael.

We put Monty and the mule to work together, dragging sheep bodies to the big pile we were making. Rafael had the notion to cover them up with dry trees and branches and grass. He dumped lamp oil on the edges and some in the center, and set it alight. But it didn't burn like he thought it would. It cooked and cooked, and at first it smelled pretty good, even though Rafael said the meat was too far gone to eat. I agreed with that, as it was getting greasy and stinky by the time we skinned out the last of them.

We kept on gathering wood and trying to keep that fire go-ing. Must have gone through a hundred trees' worth, but it didn't do any good. The fire wasn't much of one so much as it was a low, smoldering, smoky, stinky thing.

Turns out the stink was not the worst of it, nor the flies. It was the feeble burning. The cooking meat of the rotting bodies smelled rough enough to make a fella wish he didn't have a nose. I had as much fresh sheep meat as I could eat, but the smell of the turned meat put me off it, even as hungry as I was most of the time. The stink of the smoldering dead sheep didn't seem to bother Rafael at all.

I don't want to make it seem as if my time with the old man was fun or that he was pleasant to be around. It was hard work, hardest I'd ever done. And he wasn't mean, but sometimes he'd go all quiet and sad, moping around all day. He'd move so slow I was sure he'd fall over. Other times he'd set to a task and he looked ten, twenty years younger than he was.

I guessed those fits of anger and sadness all at once came on him when he thought about the boys burning his wagon, which was his home, and killing his nephew and his sheep and his dog. I know what he told Ernesto, but in my own mind I wondered if he was angry with me for the same reasons. I was one of them, a fellow from the ranch, after all.

I thought about it some at night as I laid down on the blankets Cook brought me. I didn't get too far down the trail of that topic before I fell asleep, though. I was too tired to think. Mostly I wondered about what I was going to eat for breakfast when I woke up.

Rafael was a pretty good cook and he knew how to make biscuits, which is a good thing for me, as I like biscuits. I could eat them every day, all day long.

I even told Cook that once, and he laughed and said I'd

weigh more than a prize bull and be worth half as much. I don't
know what he meant by that, but he was forever telling me to
eat everything on the plate. I never need to be told. I figured he
was mother-henning me.

Rafael, though, he never told me to eat, at least after that first
day when he brought me soup. There was something about him
and me together that was odd. It took me some time to figure it
out, but one day I did. It's because he didn't treat me like a
child who needed tending and was forever about to do
something dumb. He treated me like a man, and I liked it fine.

I know I ate like a man. Even though it was mostly sheep
meat three times a day. But I'll tell you, a fellow can only eat so
much fried-up sheep steak before he begins to recall what it was
like eating Cook's food, even if it was mostly whistleberries.

One morning, Rafael walked around and around the smoking
pile of sheep bodies, one hand rubbing on his chin—that seems
the thing to do when you are an old person and you have to
decide on something—and his injured shoulder still slumped
down on one side from where the boys had whomped on him
with an axe handle.

Cook had told him on his second visit that he really should
let him set the shoulder. I didn't understand what that meant,
but the old man shook his head no. He said it would heal itself
and he walked away. Cook looked at me with his eyebrows high,
as if he'd heard a big, old windy story and was doubtful.

Rafael's shoulder was mending, but all crooked. I asked Rafael about it one night and he did what he always did, he stared
at the fire and said nothing. I'd gotten used to hearing nothing
more than a sheep now and again and coyotes yipping near, far,
and near again. Then he spoke.

It surprised me so much when he did that. It was as if I'd
been alive a thousand years and had never heard a person's
voice before, my own included.

I looked at him and he hadn't moved, only his mouth did. The sound that came out was cracked and slow and quiet. He said, "It will remind me, this." He touched his slumped shoulder with his good hand, but didn't look at me. I believe he was talking to anybody and nobody, all at once. As if I hadn't asked a question about ten minutes before. "It will remind me that Thomas is gone and I am to carry on as I am, for him, for the sheep. And one day there will be nothing left."

I stayed awake, for a while anyway, and thought about what he said. I took it to mean he had no hope and figured he never would again. But until he died, he would have to keep on doing what he figured he was put on earth to do, day after day. I went to sleep feeling low, lower than I had since the boy died in my lap.

Anyway, I see I am as good at telling this story as I am at riding a horse, which is to say I fall off a whole lot more than I stay in the saddle. Back to what I set out to say.

Rafael walked around that stinky, smoldering pile of sheep carcasses, around and around. He stopped and still didn't look at me, but said, "Tomorrow we will drag them all to the cliff."

That was it, he said no more on the topic, so I didn't ask, even though I wanted to know how we would do that. Who was going to have to grab hold of those dead critters and tie the tow ropes onto them? And what would we do with them once we got them to the cliff? I guessed it was the ravine a ways down the canyon from where we were.

I got my answers the next morning. While he made breakfast—sheep meat and biscuits and coffee—he had me rig up the mule and the horse, and after we ate, I was up to my elbows in sheep carcass.

I thought it was funny at first. I had sheep on the inside of me and I had sheep on the outside of me. Until I lost my footing and fell knee first into the firepit. Turns out the sheep underneath weren't all blackened and crisped up like the ones around the edges where the fire had burned best.

Underneath they were goo, like if you reached into a bucket of cold porridge, but with bone beneath. I gagged some and as I flailed around trying to get back to my feet, I caught sight of Rafael. It was the first time I saw a smile on his face. I didn't see much to smile about, and it didn't get better. It was a long day of dragging death to the edge of the ravine.

We shoved the sheep over the side. Most of them rolled a few feet before snagging on a rock. I slid down on my backside and shoved them with my boots. I was stinking and covered in black soot and sheep goo and flies. It did not occur to me until late that night to ask why didn't we leave the smoldering carcasses in a pile and be done with it.

And that's what I asked Rafael the next morning at breakfast. He shook his head as he poured us both cups of coffee—another thing Cook didn't let me have. I grew to develop a taste for it, though it took some doing.

"If we don't get those sheep bodies away from this grazing ground, my sheep will never want to come here again. This I cannot have."

That's all he said. As much as I didn't want it to, it made sense to me. So I kept on with the task, foul as it was.

As a rule, I am not keen on bathing, but those nights I was happy to shuck my clothes and wade into the creek and scrub off. I used sand, as the old man said I should, and he was right. I rubbed myself raw, but it felt good. Cold, but good. I looked redder than I normally do, but I didn't care. Not like there was anybody up there to call me names.

It went on like that for three more days, me working like a dog with him working alongside me, for the most part, doing what he could with one near-useless arm. I tried to keep ahead of him, thinking of what might need doing next.

On the morning after we finished hauling the dead to the ravine, Ernesto showed up to help. If I didn't know better, I'd have thought he'd been hiding back in the trees, waiting for the worst work to get over with. But that's mean of me, because he had his own dead to deal with, and he was alone on his spread some miles to the northwest of us.

The first thing we saw of him were his sheep. Somehow, he managed to keep them moving all together. As they emerged from the sparse tree cover, I saw how he did it.

He had himself a dog. It looked like Pip, but with long black-and-white hair. That dog was busier than any animal I'd ever seen. First he'd pop up alongside one edge of the group. He'd disappear and I swear in no time he was clear along the other side, not making much noise other than low growls.

The closer they got, I'd hear his teeth snapping, and those sheep would climb up and over each other to get away from him. And do you know what else? That dog looked like he was smiling the whole time. I fancy I also heard low words and quick, sharp whistles, and I learned who made those sounds.

After a while, Ernesto rode up on that same small, spotted horse. His sheep spread out into the pasture as soon as they were run out of the trees by the dog. Rafael's sheep had worked themselves down toward the far end of the meadow, but as soon as Ernesto's sheep walked into view, they swung their heads up like somebody had whispered to them all at once to do so. A few of them stomped a front foot as if they didn't care for what they were seeing and were making their complaints heard.

I learned that Ernesto was a cousin to Rafael. I also learned he wasn't keen on having me around. I'd seen enough surly characters in my life that I knew if I ignored him, he might do the same with me. He was here to help Rafael, too, so we were stuck with each other. But he didn't view the situation that way.

I shrugged and went back to my task while he and Rafael

talked and drank coffee. I was bent over dragging a brushy-tipped branch like a short broom, raking up cinders from Rafael's wagon. I was too far from them to hear much more than a word here and there if one of them raised a voice.

"Boy," I heard behind me. I stood and turned to see Ernesto standing with his arms folded across his chest. "Rafael and I have talked. Now that I am here with my dog and my gun, you are not needed. Go back to your ranch." He said the word *ranch* like it was paining his mouth to hold it in.

"But I . . ." I was confused and looked past him at the campfire. Rafael was walking away, toward his mule. I wanted to shout to him, ask him why. But I knew why. Like always. It was time to move on. The hard work was over and now I wasn't wanted. Trouble was, I had nowhere to go.

"You have done enough. You are not needed."

I looked at my boots, and felt my ears burning. I saw Ernesto's boots and they weren't in any better shape than mine. I looked him in the eyes. If I straightened up my shoulders, which I did, I was taller than him. He was older than me, a full-grown man with a moustache and a beat-up gray felt hat with a black band pushed back on his forehead. I still didn't have a hat to cover my red wire-hair. But I decided I wasn't a child anymore. "Did Rafael say he doesn't want me around?"

Ernesto hesitated, but it was enough to let me know this was his idea and Rafael likely didn't agree with him, or didn't know he was trying to send me packing.

I nodded. "If Rafael agrees with you, I'll go away."

"You are not needed here."

But he said it to my back, because I was walking past him. "You said that already."

As I expected, the old man looked confused when I asked him if he wanted me to go away. "Dilly, you can leave when you want. But I like your help. You're a good boy." He looked from me to Ernesto, who had followed me. I looked at Ernesto. He stood with his arms folded and didn't look up. I fancy he was blushing, too.

If this is what it felt like to be bold, as Cook said I ought to be in life, I understood why he would recommend it. Still, I felt bad that Ernesto was feeling bad, if that makes sense. But I got over it quick.

Rafael spoke in quick, tight words to Ernesto in their own lingo. Ernesto tried to interrupt him once, but the old man had a head of steam built up and didn't let him get a word in. I wanted to step backward and let them at it, but I didn't dare interrupt him. He ended with, "Okay?"

Ernesto said nothing.

"Okay, I say?"

Ernesto nodded. "Okay."

"Come, Dilly, you will help me with the sheep. Ernesto will fetch his wagon."

I followed the old man as he ambled toward the far end of the meadow, where Ernesto's flock had begun to mingle with his own. He wore the revolver Cook had brought him, tucked in his trouser waistband. He was such a skinny old man that even with his wide brown leather belt, I thought his trousers might fall off him, but they never did.

"How come you didn't have a gun?"

"We did. A rifle. We used it for shooting the coyotes. When the cattle ranchers hit me, someone took it." He shrugged. "I don't know where it is now."

I felt that same guilty feeling I always got when I was reminded he'd suffered at the hands of some of my pards from the Hatterson. Other than Earl, I couldn't picture any of them acting that way. But they had, went along with Boss and did what he said. It came to me that they weren't any smarter than sheep themselves, being led here and there, told what to do, and

177

not think about any of it.

Was I like that? I reckoned I had been at times. The trick was to stop being like that. How? The old man glanced at me and broke my spell.

The dog lay in the grass before the sheep, head upright, watching everything.

"What's the dog's name?" I said.

"That is Pepe. He is the son of my Pip, you know." He smiled a little, watching the dog. "Like his mother, never takes his eyes from the sheep. He would rather watch the sheep than sleep or eat."

"Not me," I said, and I was serious. But Rafael must have thought I was joking because he laughed.

"I know that about you, Dilly. You are a big boy and if you keep on this way, you'll be a big man. But don't be big in the middle, eh?" He poked a gnarled old finger at my belly.

That was the first time he ever kidded with me. I didn't mind it. Reminded me of being with Cook, and in that moment I missed Cook about as much as I missed Granna. No, more than that, because Granna never was one for funning.

"Now, I will show you about sheep, Dilly." He looked at me. "What's the matter?"

I shrugged. "I guess I'm wondering why Ernesto doesn't like me." I figured if he was going to get his wagon, we were all going to be living there in the meadow together, and that sounded like it would be mighty uncomfortable. Like after Earl whomped on me and I still had to serve him food.

I hope Ernesto wasn't thinking about working me over, because I vowed after Earl laid into me that I would not ball up and cover myself anymore. If I am come after, I will fight back.

The old man sighed. "Ah, Ernesto, he is a good man. A proud man."

I raised my eyebrows, mostly to be polite, because it seemed

Rafael was looking for a response.

"Yes, yes. He has suffered much in this silly fight with the cattlemen. Not as much as my nephew, but enough. And he is not the only one. I have not seen many of my fellow sheepherders in some time, but Ernesto, he makes the rounds, and brings me news when he used to bring us supplies. Everywhere the cattle ranchers are fighting with the sheepherders. It is not here." He thumped his wooden staff against the hard ground.

The dog looked up at him briefly, and back to the sheep.

"A shepherd needs a dog. Sheep will roam, sometimes alone, others in groups. The reason they did not leave us when we brought Thomas to his resting place, I cannot say. Perhaps it is because they were tired from being beaten by the cattle ranchers the night before. At least that was helpful."

The sheep numbered a few hundred, and Rafael said, "You know, not many of us Basques learned how to watch over the sheep back in our home country. This is something we learn once we get here. Many ranchers wish to have sheep and use this open land, but they don't have anyone to watch over their sheep. We do this, me and my cousins, west of here, in Idaho."

He shook his head at the memory, and looked out across the sheep toward something I couldn't see. "But always we save our money so one day we might buy our own land. This place, Wyoming, is good land for sheep, good for families, lots of land for sale and much open range land, too. So we bought land near this range. You saw the land I own, eh?"

I nodded, thinking it looked a whole lot like this land.

"We build up our own sheep herds. I knew that one day we will have a ranch of our own, me and my nephew. With Ernesto and other cousins and friends on their own lands nearby, we can all share the work. And send for our families."

"I'm sorry it didn't work out that way, Rafael. What will you do now?"

He looked at me as if I had snakes for hair.

"I will do nothing different. I am here and Thomas is here and Ernesto and the others. We will not be chased off our own land. Or," he held up a thick finger. "From land meant for all." He smacked the ground again with his staff.

There wasn't much else a fellow could say to that, so I kept my mouth quiet. I admired his intention to stick it out, though.

He spent the rest of the day telling me things about sheep. Mostly that they aren't as dumb as I thought. And they're friendly. Well, some of them, anyway. And the young ones like to have a lot of fun, romping and jumping up and down and playing with the other young ones. About like regular children, I expect.

As we were walking back toward camp from circling the far end of the meadow, I said, "Rafael, what's it like where you come from?"

This caught him by surprise because we hadn't talked much for a while. Now here I was asking him about his home country. It was his turn to surprise me because he said, "It is a beautiful place, so special it cannot be contained by Spain or by France." As he said this, he puffed out his chest.

"We have mountains, great mountains, but it is green there. And we have the ocean. Many Basques are great fishermen." He stopped talking and rubbed his chin. I thought he was going to say more, but he didn't.

That was the way with him, I learned. You could be having what you thought was a conversation one minute, and the next he'd gaze off toward something I couldn't see and he'd get all quiet. I figured he'd pick up where he left off when he got tired of looking at the view.

That old man surprised me again, like I knew he would. "And you? What is your home like, Dilly?"

Now that was a question I had never been asked, let alone

pondered before. Finally, I said the truth. "I don't have one."

"You must have a home, Dilly. We all are from somewhere."

"Oh, I come from Ohio, but I don't have a special fondness for it. No kin, no memories that stuck with me as useful or important, really."

"Where is the place you like best?"

Now see, there was another of those questions I never gave thought to. I shrugged. I thought back on my train rides and journeying by myself from town to town, always hungry and run off by dogs and people who thought I was looking to do them harm. I thought about Ohio, Iowa, Colorado, but none of it stuck with me as a place I could claim I was fond of. "That might be around these parts, I guess. Good as any."

Rafael nodded. "This is your home." He rapped that staff on the ground again. A nearby young sheep kicked up its feet and danced off. We both laughed a little at that.

CHAPTER TWENTY-THREE

I'd like to say that me and Ernesto became friendly once he returned the next day, his sheep wagon towed by two mules, but no. We gave each other nods and when we had to set to a task together, it was in silence. He wasn't what you'd call mean, but there was no friendliness between us.

I tried to keep in mind that he was the old man's kin, after all. And he gave many kindnesses to Rafael. The first was insisting the old man sleep in the sheep wagon while he stayed outside across the fire from me. Even that didn't much bother me because I dozed off not long after we ate, what with the snapping fire and the belly full of food.

One thing I didn't mind about having Ernesto out there was his singing. He'd hum and sing songs, low and quiet, as if to himself, all in his native tongue, but I could hear them fine. I have no idea what he was singing about, but I liked hearing it all the same. Made me feel safe as I drifted to sleep.

Of course, I wished during the day it could have been different between us, but as Cook once told me one day, when I told him I wished I didn't have such bold ears, "If wishes were horses, beggars would ride." I did not understand that until I thought on it while working one hot afternoon with Rafael and Ernesto. I reckoned it meant nothing comes easy.

A couple of days after Ernesto brought his sheep and wagon over, we were inspecting all the sheep for wounds, mostly because Ernesto insisted on it. Rafael winked at me as if he was

182

letting Ernesto think he was getting away with something. I sided with Rafael—if the sheep had any lingering wounds from the attack, surely we would have seen them acting funny or odd.

The dog, Pepe, was earning his keep that day, I tell you. He ran here and there and back again, all without losing that wide, sloppy-tongued grin. Most of the sheep were fine, of course, but I had to admit, Ernesto was right. Some of them had taken a licking on their heads and the bloodied spots attracted the flies something awful.

I fetched water and Ernesto washed the cuts clean, picking out dirt and squirming bugs. Rafael ground up handfuls of damp sage and pressed it into the cuts, and smeared the whole thing on top with mud. It must not have felt too good because none of those sheep were too excited about it. They kicked and bleated and carried on, but we held them tight.

"Won't that mud make them sicker?" I asked.

Rafael shrugged. "My medicines burned and Ernesto has none now. This will do."

I think over time I impressed Ernesto because I was strong and did whatever needed doing without complaining. Not that I didn't want to. But Rafael's arm was still not in very good shape and it seemed like they needed help. Also, even if I wanted to, I couldn't leave until I talked with Cook again.

If he was going to see his sister soon, I could tag along like he'd offered. I couldn't think of much else I'd like better than traveling with Cook. Of course, I'd miss Rafael and Pepe.

After we finished checking over the last of the sheep, Ernesto nodded and the dog low-crawled round the edge of the herd, keeping them in hand and looking nervous. I wouldn't want to be a sheep around ol' Pepe.

Ernesto stretched his back and said that since the day was still young, we were going to move the sheep to a new grazing ground. My first thought was that Cook wouldn't be able to find us. He didn't seem all that keen on direction anyway. Rafael must have seen my worried look, because he said, "It isn't far. Your big friend will find us, Dilly."

This was news to Ernesto. "Who is this big friend?" His eyes were wide and he looked from one of us to the other.

"He means my friend, Cook. He's brought us flour and beans and such."

"Bah," he said, walking away, his face tight and his eyes narrowed. "Another from the ranch." He began breaking down camp and getting the wagon ready to move.

Rafael shrugged and patted my shoulder. "Your Cook will find us, Dilly. Do not worry. All he has to do is listen for Ernesto's sputtering." He grinned at me and we all pitched in to ready the camp for the move.

As Ernesto wished, we uprooted ourselves and set up in a fresh meadow not far to the east that Rafael said he hadn't used since late the summer before. It had more lumps and rolls to it, so Rafael said we'd have to take turns keeping "a good eye," as he called it, lest the sheep wander off when we weren't looking.

As it happens, I needn't have worried about Cook. I kept looking for him, and after a couple of days I ran out of excuses to go back to the old meadow to look for something that wasn't there.

I even thought of laying out an arrow on the ground made of rocks or logs, something to point the way to our new camp for Cook. But I worried that it might tip off some cattle rancher looking for a tussle with the sheepmen, so I didn't do it.

On the third afternoon following our move, Ernesto said he had to ride his spotted pony to Greenhaven for supplies. Along the way he was going to help other of their friends, one a sheepman to the northwest, another to the north, with their herds. He glanced at me, but only when he said the sheep would need protecting. And he asked if Rafael would prefer his rifle to the revolver.

"No," said the old man. "We will be fine. You may need it. And when you return, we shall have a feast, eh?"

I was pleased that I'd be alone with Rafael again, at least for a few days. And also because he was happier than he'd been since I got to know him. Ernesto nodded, readied his gear, and left with a quick wave over his shoulder.

Pepe watched him leave, but Ernesto must have sensed it because he looked at the dog from across the pasture and said something I could not make out. The dog went back to the sheep, but I saw his head turn every few seconds until Ernesto was out of sight.

The rest of the afternoon passed quietly. It was hot and the sheep did what they always do, they ate. The dog dozed and circled, depending on which minute I looked over at him. Even Rafael took to snoozing in the shade of the sheep wagon. I admit I may have napped a minute or two myself.

It was that night I learned happiness never lasts.

CHAPTER TWENTY-FOUR

That night, after we ate, I lay back and watched as the sky purpled, with long streaks of silver clouds looking like they were painted up there by giants. I could hear sheep not far from camp, and I knew Pepe was keeping an eye on them. Monty and Lucky the mule were tied close by for the night, along with Ernesto's mules.

"Rafael?"

"Hmm?" He poked at the coals with a stick.

"What do you think is going to happen with me next?"

"I do not understand what you mean by 'next.'"

"I guess . . . I guess I'm not sure."

He nodded and kept poking the fire. We both watched the glowing orange coals as night slowly came. He said, "If you are worried about your friend, Cook, he will not forget you. You will know when it is time to go or to stay." He looked at me. "You are welcome to stay with me, Dilly. I can promise there will always be work, eh?" He smiled and so did I.

"Thank you," I said. It was a kind thing for him to offer and something I did not expect. I thought of Ernesto and that soured the idea a little. I got to thinking about Cook again and figured we'd see him the next day, for certain. After all, he was a busy man.

I fell asleep with that happy thought in my head. Then loud huffing and pounding sounds woke me.

As will happen when you first wake up, I was confused. The

night was black, what moon there was had clouded over, but I heard sounds and as I widened my eyes, I saw far-off dancing lights. It took me a few seconds to recognize them as torches. A pair of them, moving closer.

"Rafael!" I shouted and ran to the wagon, but he was not inside. That's when I heard gunshots and saw a flash burst from the barrel of a gun a dozen yards before me. It was Rafael, shooting at something. Or someone.

My eyes saw more in the night now. The pounding came from horses and their torch-carrying riders, thundering in close. I ran to Rafael, who stood before me, his back to me, the revolver raised in his left hand. He fired again and shouted something, a word I did not recognize. It was the first time I heard him shout.

"Rafael!"

He turned his head and saw me. "Dilly! Get away from here! Go . . . run!"

"No, I can help!" I did not know how, but there had to be something I could do. I ran to the wagon and found the axe handle. Where I'd left Rafael standing, I saw bright bursts from guns close together, one higher than the other. Rafael and a rider.

I didn't slow my pace. With a couple more strides I saw it was Earl on the horse, and Earl who'd shot. He'd shot . . .

"Rafael?" I didn't see him standing, and there he was, on the ground, on his back.

I ran to him and stumbled to my knees. I grabbed his shirtfront and shook him but his head flopped. "Rafael!" I screamed his name, shaking him. He didn't respond. He couldn't. He'd been shot by Earl. Shot dead.

"You!" I shouted up at the man on the horse. "What did you do!"

"You're next . . . friend!" He held his torch and reins in one hand, a revolver in the other, aimed at me.

The second horse stepped forward and the rider shouted, "I told you to tend to the sheep!"

It was Boss. But Earl didn't want to take his eyes from me.

"The sheep, fool!"

That broke the moment. Earl growled as he swung his horse and galloped away.

"Still here, you filthy foundling?" Boss slid down out of the saddle. "I took you in, even though I could tell by looking at you that you were trash, never would amount to a thing. And I was right, look at you! Taking sides with sheepmen! I should have let you starve, then kicked you out for the wolves to finish."

Even in the dark I saw his red face and wide, white eyes, and bared teeth as he walked toward me. *Off his bean*, I kept thinking. Cook would say he was off his bean. He hated me, and I hated him with everything I was. He held a gun on me, and with his other hand, threw his torch. It whipped through the air like a comet, spinning end over end past me. It didn't reach the wagon.

From the dark to my right, the second torch jumped and bobbed in the night, then came back toward us. Then the horse and rider, carrying that torch, pounded by behind me.

It was Earl, and he howled a cross between a war cry and laughter. In seconds the night bloomed bright. Over my shoulder I saw the sheep wagon erupt in flame. Earl cackled and rode off, loosing gunshots into the air and shouting. From behind me, the night burned bright and hot.

"Time to follow your vermin friend, boy. Time teach you a lesson." Boss smiled as he said it.

I didn't care that he had that gun aimed at me. I would drive him into the ground like a fence post. I hefted the axe handle he'd given me as I lunged to my feet, swinging the handle high and screaming.

"Boss! No!"

I looked toward the voice. It didn't seem possible, but in the pulsing heat and light, I saw Cook, his big shape looking even bigger in the firelight.

The wagon's blaze made his dark face look like some kind of devil. No, that's not it. It was his eyes, almost like they were glowing. He didn't look at me, though. He looked at Boss. And he had a rifle pointed at him, too. Boss guessed I was no harm, so he swung his revolver off me and at Cook.

I heard Cook shout, "Boss! No!" I shouted the same thing. I tried to reach Boss but I was too late. I threw the axe handle, but all I heard was the awful booming of guns, too close and too loud and too bright in the dark night. The axe handle caught Boss in the backside but he was already spinning.

I saw his left side jerk as if someone shoved him hard on the shoulder. He grabbed at his gut and took a long, odd step forward toward Cook, then another. He kept that pistol up, though.

I heard Cook shout, "Boss, no! That's enough!"

Boss had a funny look on his face. His eyes opened big, like he was surprised, and his mouth was wide. But he kept that pistol up and pointed at Cook, straight and true, and his thumb pulled back on the hammer and I ran at him, shouting, "Stop it!"

He turned his head and looked at me once more. His mouth got big like he was going to take a bite of something and he swung his pistol around at me again. *Fine,* I thought. *At least it's not at Cook.*

"Dilly, no!" Cook shouted. "Get down!"

I saw what was going to happen and there was nothing I could do about it. Cook shot Boss again, as Boss was about to shoot me. Boss jerked to one side, kept going, and collapsed on the short, dung-messed grass the sheep had nibbled down to almost nothing.

His gun hit the ground, butt first, and I guess his finger was still on the trigger because it went off. I don't think it hit anybody because it was aimed too high, as if Boss was trying to shoot out the stars.

I turned to see Cook holding his rifle, but it was slowly aiming itself down, down to point at the ground. Then all of Cook was headed that way. That's when I saw something was wrong. I shoved up off my knees and ran to him, shouting, "Cook! Cook!"

He dropped hard on his right knee, his big body swaying like the top of a tall tree in a windstorm.

"Cook!" I shouted again and fell against him.

He swayed, dropped his rifle, and grabbed me hard. "S'okay, s'okay, Dilly."

But I knew it wasn't, because he'd been shot in the middle of his big belly.

He saw it, too. "Ruined my good apron." Cook smiled and looked up at me, too slow, though.

I wanted to kid with him, tell him it was his only apron, which of course meant that it was also his good one. But it didn't work that way.

I heard a horse thundering away but paid it no mind.

"Followed Boss and Earl here. Too late . . . only ones who wouldn't listen."

"It's okay, Cook. It's all right now."

"Pay attention now, Dilly. Got my sister in Washington. Her whereabouts . . . in my things. You go to her, explain all this. She'll take you in."

"No," I said. "Cook, you're going to be okay!" I was holding his shoulder, squeezing it like he did to me. My other hand rubbed his big cheek, all bristly from his curly beard.

"Sure I am, Dilly. Sure I am. Ain't no worries for me now.

You got to promise me to take care, Dilly, okay?"

"Okay, Cook, but you're going to be okay, you're going to be fine."

But he wasn't fine. Was never going to be again.

We sat, with Cook leaning against me. I don't know how long. We talked, mostly I talked, Cook's breathing hurt him some. I didn't know what to do. Water, I thought I'd get him water, but as I got up he held onto my arm, so I stayed with him.

I wanted to go for help, but who was there? I'd been here for weeks and I didn't even know where I was, in some meadow somewhere. I didn't even know where the ranch was.

I saw nothing in the night that was moving. I called and called, but other than the crackle of flame and the bleat of a sheep, I heard nothing.

I stayed that way, talking and holding Cook, for hours. For the rest of the long night, while the wagon burned. I never fell asleep once. Then I noticed I could see things.

I looked down at Cook. I could tell by his eyes he was dead. They looked up, past me, past anything you can see on earth, up through the smoke, into the gray sky.

"Cook?" I rubbed his cheek again, and held him tighter. He was a big man but so am I, and I pulled him close once more. I felt his beard against my own beardless face for the first time. I remember thinking that's what hugging your own papa feels like, all scratchy. But there should be a big belly laugh after that. Not nothing.

I don't know how long I stayed that way, rocking Cook and telling him over and over he'd be okay. I wanted to believe that if I said something enough, it would come to pass. "It's okay, Cook, it's okay, all of it's going to be okay now."

After a while I felt something touch me on the shoulder. It kept up and I looked up. It was Ernesto. He was patting me with his fingertips on the shoulder.

I saw he'd been crying, too. I remembered Rafael.

"Close his eyes now, boy." He nodded.

I looked at him again, shaking my head like I did not understand.

He knelt before me. "Close his eyes," and nodded again.

Letting go of Cook was the hardest thing I have ever done. Harder than anything else, ever. Harder than watching Franklin go, harder than leaving the Torbenhast farm, harder than seeing my Granna dead.

"Is this how it's always going to be?" I didn't know I'd said it out loud. I wasn't even sure what I meant, but Ernesto must have, because he shook his head.

"No." He rested a hand on my shoulder and looked back toward the smoldering wreck of the wagon, at the dead old man. His old friend, Rafael. "Only sometimes."

EPILOGUE

Autumn, 1931
Big Horn County, Wyoming

It was all my fault, of course, the whole mess. Not Boss's fight with the sheepmen, but Cook and Boss dying, the old man Rafael, and maybe his nephew, too, though I don't know for sure about him. Earl did that to him and I wished I could have done the same to Earl. Especially after I came to know the old man.

Over the following months and years, more of Rafael's family came to America from Basque Country, their homeland, here to our valley. And they bought sheep and helped each other, bought land together and brought more of their families here. And more Basque families bought more sheep and more land. And while that was going on, a funny thing happened. The cattle farmers started running sheep, too.

It's true. I'd like to say this was caused by something other than an urge for money, but I would be lying. Sheep are natural grubbers, and in this land are more practical critters to keep, as they will eat much of what the cattle won't, namely sage and shrubs. They also breed faster, and their offspring mature faster. And all that means money. That doesn't mean raising sheep is an easy thing. There's disease and predators and plain bad luck that come along on a regular basis.

We've had tough years, to be sure, but one that stands out is the hard winter of 1898–1899. Some cattlemen were wiped out in the blizzards. Their cattle froze and died by the thousands.

Most all the sheep made it through, being fighters, because they ate the tops off the sage and grubbed down to eat the grass beneath the sage plants. After that, a number of cattlemen put on more sheep.

I guess they learned what I came to learn, working with Ernesto. Sheep aren't much of a danger to cattle. It's true they eat the grass down closer to the ground, but that means you have to keep them moving. They're different. No more different than sheepmen are to cattlemen, once they figure out how to live on the same range. It took a while, longer than it should have, and with more blood and tears shed than I have mentioned in these pages, but it eventually happened here, and in other places in Wyoming, and throughout the West, as well.

Yes, I did come to know Ernesto, and found him to be as good a friend and, I hope, me to him, as I ever did find in life. Who would have thought from our rocky beginnings we would grow close? Not that he couldn't be a surly rig now and again. I reckon we all can claim the same.

He is an old man now, older than Rafael was when we lost him. But Ernesto is still with us and I am still learning from him. I like to say he has forgotten more about sheep and people (and singing) than I could ever learn. He tells me to stop with the foolishness. But he puffs up when I say it.

One of the people who came to America from what Ernesto calls "home" is Rafael's great-niece, Felice. She was cousin to Thomas, the boy who died in my lap. I never mentioned much of that night to her, but she must have been told by Ernesto or somebody else.

Anyway, she was a pretty girl, prettier even than Myra. I helped her learn to speak English, which is a funny thing, when you think on it. Me, Dilly, teaching anybody anything. But it must have worked, because I can understand her. Oddly, I also began to learn how to speak Euskara, her native language. I guess that will happen if you spend enough time with somebody.

We ended up marrying once we got a little age on us. I think she's a year older than me, I don't really know. It's not something that ever came up. We helped Ernesto build a house, and we lived there with him for a spell.

We got a late start on it, but we have been lucky to have two children of our own, young Constanza, who is herself married to a fine young man, even if he is not Basque, named Jacob, and they expect a child of their own any day now. We also had a son, young Clarence (namesake of Cook), who died of a sudden fever and illness when he was but five. We still miss him so.

The old ranch, the Hatterson, changed hands twice in all those years since that night Boss died. The first was when Myra, his daughter, sold the place to one of Boss's friends. You might recall Delahanty. He used it mostly for the land, to run extra cattle. I made a last trip back there with Boss's body on the back of his own horse. They buried him in the family cemetery on a rise behind the big house. Myra was thankful, but I did not do it for her or for Boss. I did it so I could retrieve Cook's things, which I found in the cookshack.

Everything there smelled of him, reminded me of him. It was difficult. Nobody bothered me. I went back to the meadow. By then, Pepe the dog had made a belly-crawling return, and soon enough was back to tending his sheep. We'd only lost two in the attack.

Me and Ernesto loaded Cook and Rafael onto the younger mules and we brought them back to Rafael's place, where we buried them atop that knoll where Thomas lay. I visit with all three of them when the mood moves me.

It took some time, but I finally sent a letter to Cook's sister and a small bundle of his things, a pocket watch, papers and letters, and a photograph of a pretty woman I like to think is someone he once loved. I kept his old Barlow pocketknife for myself. I have it with me now, but I still can't peel a potato in one go like he could.

I say bringing Boss's body home was a last trip, but that's not the truth of it. I also said the Hatterson Ranch changed hands twice in those years since. The second time was when me and Felice bought it, must be fifteen years ago now. Yep. Delahanty's children had enough of the ranching life. They sold it all and the last I heard, they made for San Francisco. I think that's where Myra went, too.

I don't think of her often, but once in a while I'll walk into the kitchen and find myself turning red at the memory of what I saw, all those years ago, in that very room. It was innocent enough, I suppose, but I don't know. I also recall those green socks she made for me. I wish her well.

I am finishing the writing of this from her father's office. I was pleased to find that even with the various inhabitants, most of his books had been left here. I have spent the years since slowly working my way through them. Some of them are entertaining, such as anything by Charles Dickens, but others, Racine's *Treatise on the Economics and Ethics of Animal Husbandry* comes to mind, take all my strength to turn the page.

Let's see . . . as to Earl, I never did hear what happened to him beyond that night when he turned tail. The day I brought Boss home, one of the hands told me the last any of them saw of Earl, he was riding westward, hell-for-leather. Good riddance. I hope he rode straight into the ocean and drowned.

People like that don't usually end up well anyway, though I doubt my ill wishes will hasten him along. I expect if he's dead, he's in a constant battle of fisticuffs with old Farmer Torbenhast. I chuckle at the thought of the two of them, huffing and cursing and blacking each other's eyes day after day for eternity.

As to catching you up on my life, I am afraid I was a mite windier than I expected I would be. When I first was found by you at the ranch gate that summer morning, I was not yet thirteen years old. You seemed so much older than me, but now that I think back on it, you surely weren't but ten years my senior. Even after these forty-odd years, that should put you still among the living, if you have lived a life free of mishap. I do hope so, Franklin.

I take heart on that point because a number of years ago, you wrote to me, general delivery, from Hawaii. A place called Kauai. You explained how after you left the Hatterson, you rode for the coast, worked your way across the Pacific on a steamship. You liked it so much you stayed on and started a school, then ended up marrying a local woman and fathering a half-dozen children.

You said you were happy. You also said you heard from Clement, who knew somebody else who worked on a freighter hauling, of all things, sheep to Hawaii. You wrote that you were relieved I ended up on the good side.

I always intended to write back to you. As a matter of fact, I did write a letter, I never mailed it. I wasn't certain you'd want to hear from me, after what I said to you that day of your leaving. I hope you know I hold only the fondest thoughts for you.

And so, I am putting all this down as a hello and a thank you, a handshake in thought, if I may be so poetic. I hope it reaches you.

If you care to, and if you aren't still sore with me for what I said, you can write me at the same place you last saw me. I don't guess I got all that far. But sometimes it seems like I have traveled a lifetime to get here. And I reckon I have at that.

Your friend,
Dilly

A Note from the Author

from Basque Country their homeland in north-central Spain and southwest France. Today, the Basque influence in America is well-enriching far beyond sheepherding, and the Basque culture can be experienced in cities and communities throughout the West in areas such as Wyoming, Idaho, Nevada, and Cali...

A NOTE FROM THE AUTHOR

Although *Dilly* is a work of fiction, the attacks depicted in the story are modest compared with the all-too-real Sheep Wars, a series of brutal conflicts that took place throughout the American West in the latter part of the nineteenth and early twentieth centuries.

Cattlemen regarded the increasing use of public grazing lands by sheepherders and their flocks as invasions on acreage they had long used to graze their cattle. More than 120 violent interactions from 1870 to 1920 between the two groups resulted in the deaths of fifty-four sheepherders and more than 100,000 sheep (anecdotal evidence suggests much higher figures).

Wyoming's deadliest attack on sheepherders, the Spring Creek Raid, took place on April 2, 1909. Two sheepmen were shot to death, two others escaped, two sheep wagons were burned, and twenty-four sheep were shot. Though the raid was brutal, it is also notable for the fact that five of the seven attackers were arrested and sent to prison, marking the first successful prosecution of sheep raiders in Wyoming. The raid was also the last in which shepherds were murdered in Wyoming, though it was not the last sheep attack in that state's history—two more followed in 1911 and 1912.

Despite its bloody past, sheep ranching in the West has become a widespread, respected occupation. Notable among sheepherders are the Basques, who in the mid-nineteenth century brought to the United States a rich cultural heritage from Basque Country, their homeland in north-central Spain and southwest France. Today, the Basque influence in America is vast, stretching far beyond sheepherding, and the Basque culture can be experienced in thriving communities throughout the West, in states such as Wyoming, Idaho, Nevada, and California.

—MPM

ABOUT THE AUTHOR

Matthew P. Mayo is an award-winning author of novels and short stories. His novel, *Stranded: A Story of Frontier Survival* (Five Star), won the Western Heritage Wrangler Award, the Spur Award, the Peacemaker Award, and the Willa Award, among others. He and his wife, videographer Jennifer Smith-Mayo, along with their trusty pup/trail scout, Miss Tess, rove the byways of North America in search of hot coffee, tasty whiskey, and high adventure. For more information, drop by Matthew's website at MatthewMayo.com.

The employees of Five Star Publishing hope you have enjoyed this book.

Our Five Star novels explore little-known chapters from America's history, stories told from unique perspectives that will entertain a broad range of readers.

Other Five Star books are available at your local library, bookstore, all major book distributors, and directly from Five Star/Gale.

Connect with Five Star Publishing

Visit us on Facebook:
https://www.facebook.com/FiveStarCengage

Email:
FiveStar@cengage.com

For information about titles and placing orders:
(800) 223-1244
gale.orders@cengage.com

To share your comments, write to us:
Five Star Publishing
Attn: Publisher
10 Water St., Suite 310
Waterville, ME 04901